The Courageous Cats Compete

Here are two more fast-moving stories starring the five r   ^ ..
Courageous (

D1584721

Talent .

There's fierce competition among the cats when Clive organizes some sporting events. Camilla is able to show off her talents but Tiger is left feeling worthless. He organizes a contest of his own which has some very surprising results!

Stars in Their Eyes

When one of the cats is chosen to star in a TV programme the fur really begins to fly! The cats fall out as fame and fortune become more important than friendship. Is this the end of the Courageous Cats' Club?

Steve Wood has worked for many years as a writer for children's television and theatre, and he is also an experienced actor and presenter. When Steve is not working, he enjoys trying to play golf. He lives near Manchester.

Text copyright © 2006 Steve Wood
Illustrations copyright © 2006 Woody Fox
This edition copyright © 2006 Lion Hudson

The moral rights of the author and illustrator
have been asserted

A Lion Children's Book
an imprint of
Lion Hudson plc
Mayfield House, 256 Banbury Road,
Oxford OX2 7DH, England
www.lionhudson.com
ISBN-13: 978-0-7459-6011-1
ISBN-10: 0-7459-6011-1

First edition 2006
1 3 5 7 9 10 8 6 4 2 0

A catalogue record for this book is available
from the British Library

Typeset in 14/18 Baskerville MT Schoolbook
Printed and bound in Great Britain
by Cox and Wyman Ltd, Reading

The Courageous Cats Compete

Steve Wood

Illustrations by Woody Fox

LI🐾N
CHILDREN'S

Talent Show

Contents

1

Watching

The young sparrow fluttered onto the lawn and pecked at the bits of bread scattered all over the grass. The little bird was surprised that none of his friends were tucking into this feast – usually there was fierce competition for every crumb on offer, but there wasn't another bird in sight. The young sparrow didn't know it was being watched. Hiding in the bushes at the edge of the lawn were the five members of the Courageous Cats' Club!

The leader of the club was Clive, a scruffy old black cat with big eyes and big legs. He used to have a big tail too. Sadly, it had to be removed after an accident, but that's another story. Clive had given up chasing birds a long time ago. He was a lot slower than he used to be and he didn't want the others to make fun of him.

Next to Clive was Douglas. He was a Manx cat from the Isle of Man, and like most Manx cats he was born without a tail. That didn't stop him from being quick on his feet. He knew he could catch the bird if he wanted to, but it was only a baby and it didn't seem a very fair contest.

Next to Douglas was Bertie, a fat white cat with large patches of red, cream and black fur. Around his eyes, perfect circles of black fur gave the impression that he wore glasses. Bertie wasn't interested in chasing birds – it required far too much energy. Instead he was daydreaming – he was trying to imagine what it would be like if people fed cats like they fed birds. He licked his lips at the thought of waking up every morning to find bits of fish lying around the garden.

Next to Bertie was Camilla, a beautiful cat whose fur was the colour of clotted cream. Camilla loved chasing birds and was eager to make the sparrow her next victim. She lowered her sleek, slender body close to the ground. Then, ever so slowly, she moved forward. Ever so quietly, she advanced on her prey. The bell

fastened to her collar didn't make a sound –
Camilla was an expert in silent stalking. She
moved closer and closer to the sparrow, which
was nibbling on a crust.

Tiger held his breath. He was the youngest
member of the club – a small kitten with lovely
soft ginger fur. He never chased birds. The only
things he chased were bumblebees, but he'd
never caught one and if he had he would
probably have let it go.

Tiger hardly dared look as Camilla edged
onto the lawn. The little sparrow had no idea

she was there. Camilla prepared to pounce. In a few seconds it would be over. In a few seconds the little bird would be dead.

Tiger knew he would have to act fast if he was going to help the bird to escape.

2

Who is the Greatest?

Tiger ran onto the lawn.

'Go for it, Camilla!' he shouted.

Instantly, the sparrow flew away. Camilla was furious.

'What did you do that for?' she yelled. 'I was just about to catch that bird!'

'Sorry,' said Tiger.

'You did it on purpose! You frightened it away so it wouldn't get hurt! You're a big baby!'

The other cats emerged from the bushes and sat on the grass.

'Leave Tiger alone,' said Clive. 'You know he doesn't like it when we chase birds.'

'What do you mean, *we*?' snapped Camilla. 'I'm the only one who goes after them and we all know why! Because none of you can catch them!'

'I could have caught that bird if I'd wanted to,' said Douglas.

'So could I,' said Bertie.

Camilla laughed. '*You*? To catch a bird you need to be an all-round athlete like me.'

'I *am* an all-round athlete,' said Bertie. 'Well… perhaps I'm not an athlete, but I am all round.'

Clive, Douglas and Tiger laughed, but Camilla was in no mood for jokes.

'Let's have a bird-chasing competition,' she said.

'No,' said Tiger. 'Chasing birds is cruel.'

'It's not cruel,' said Camilla. 'It's natural. We're cats and we chase birds.'

'We don't *have* to,' insisted Tiger.

Camilla ignored Tiger's protest. 'A bird-chasing competition would be fun,' she said. 'And it will prove who is the greatest athlete.'

'Just because you can catch a bird doesn't

mean you're a great athlete,' said Douglas.
'To be a great athlete you need to demonstrate
speed, strength, endurance and agility.'

'Quite right,' said Clive. 'A bird-chasing
competition won't prove anything.'

'Let's have an athletics competition!' said
Tiger, who was eager to make sure no birds
came to any harm.

Bertie groaned. 'That sounds even *more*
exhausting.'

'It will do you good,' said Camilla. 'You could
do with losing some weight.'

'We'll have lots of events,' said Tiger. 'To test
our speed and strength and… what were the
other things, Douglas?'

'Endurance and agility.'

'What are they?'

'Endurance is when you can keep going over long distances and agility is being swift and nimble.'

'We'll test all those things,' said Tiger. 'I'll organize the events and – '

'Just a minute,' said Clive. 'If there's any organizing to be done, I'm the one to do it. I'm the leader of the club, remember?'

Clive got to his feet and paced around the garden. He was quickly thinking how he could wriggle out of the sporting contest.

'Such an event will involve a great deal of planning,' he said. 'It will require the brains of an experienced organizer like me. I'm prepared to make the necessary arrangements, but unfortunately it will mean I won't be able to take part.'

Clive did his best to look heartbroken.

'I could organize it and take part as well,' said Tiger.

'No, no, no,' said Clive. 'You're underestimating the size of the task.'

'No, I'm not.'

'Yes, you are!' shouted Clive.

Tiger jumped at the harshness of Clive's voice. Douglas, Camilla and Bertie were shocked too – Clive rarely lost his temper with Tiger.

Clive suddenly felt guilty about shouting at his little friend.

'Believe me Tiger, it's a huge job,' he said gently. 'So huge, I'll probably need you to be my assistant.'

'Really?' Tiger's right ear began to twitch, which it always did when he was excited.

'You can be the scorekeeper,' said Clive. 'It's a very important job.'

'I'll be the best scorekeeper ever,' said Tiger. 'And I'm going to take part in all the events as well.'

'When are we having the contest?' asked Douglas.

'Tomorrow,' said Clive. 'All Courageous Cats to meet at ten o'clock in the usual place.'

Tiger jumped to his feet. 'I'm going home to practise my speed and strength and endurance and… that other thing.'

'Agility,' said Camilla. She stood up and wandered to the middle of the lawn. 'It's what you need if you want to be able to do this!'

Suddenly, Camilla sprang high into the air and swiped her claws at a blackbird that was passing overhead. The bird let out a squawk and crashed into the garden fence.

'Now I'll show you how to finish the job.'

Camilla sprinted towards the bird, which was lying on the ground, quivering.

'Leave it alone!' shouted Tiger.

Camilla stopped. 'Why?' she asked. 'Do *you* want to do it?'

Tiger stared at the bird. It was barely moving now.

'Go on,' said Camilla. 'Once you've killed your first bird, you'll want to do it all the time.'

'Don't do anything you don't want to do, Tiger,' said Douglas.

'Go on,' said Camilla. 'I'll never call you a baby again.'

Tiger ran to the bird and grabbed it in his mouth.

'Now you're behaving like a real cat!' shouted Camilla.

Tiger darted into the bushes with the bird between his teeth.

3

The Contestants Gather

All the cats were up and about bright and early the following morning. All except for Bertie. He decided the best way to prepare for the athletics contest was to sleep in.

Clive made his way to the apple tree in Bertie's garden – the official meeting place of the Courageous Cats' Club. There he sat down and rehearsed his speech for the opening ceremony.

Meanwhile, Camilla was in her garden, warming up with a series of stretching exercises. It was very hot and normally she would have been looking forward to a spot of sunbathing, but Camilla was taking the contest very seriously.

Douglas prepared by going for a light jog. As

he passed through Tiger's garden, he spotted
the little cat rummaging in a dustbin bag. Tiger
had ripped it open and rubbish was scattered all
over the place.

'Hi Tiger,' shouted Douglas.

Tiger immediately stopped what he was doing.
He jumped onto a garden bench and sat down.

'It's not like you to look for scraps,' said
Douglas. He joined Tiger on the bench. 'Have
you not had any breakfast?'

Tiger didn't answer.

'It's not a good idea to face the athletics competition on an empty stomach.'

Still Tiger didn't speak, and Douglas sensed he was upset.

'Do you want to have a chat about what happened yesterday?' he asked.

Tiger shook his head.

'I can understand if you're angry with Camilla. She only caught that bird to annoy you and there's no way you would have killed it if she hadn't teased you.'

'I don't want to talk about it,' said Tiger quietly.

'OK,' said Douglas. 'Come on, it's nearly time for the competition to begin.'

The two cats jumped to the ground and made their way through the neighbouring gardens to Bertie's place. They spotted Clive sitting beneath the apple tree, talking to himself.

'Hi Clive,' shouted Douglas.

'Good morning,' said Clive. 'Are you ready for action?'

'I certainly am.'

'And is my assistant ready to take on his important role?'

'Yes,' said Tiger. 'I've been practising my adding up.'

Camilla was next to arrive. She nodded to the others as she strode across the lawn to the apple tree. She stood on her hind legs, sank her front claws into the trunk and enjoyed a long slow stretch.

At this moment Bertie squeezed through the cat flap in the kitchen door and ambled down the long garden.

'Am I late?' he said. 'Have I missed any of the races?'

'No,' said Tiger.

'What a shame,' said Bertie quietly.

'Gather round, everybody,' said Clive trying to sound important.

The others did as they had been instructed.

'It is my duty as Chief of the Courageous Cats' Club Competition Committee to get things under way by making a speech.'

'Here we go,' muttered Bertie. He lay down and made himself comfortable – Clive's speeches had been known to go on for some time.

'I will start by informing you of the rules,' said Clive. 'There are only two of them. Rule number one: No cat shall be caught cheating.'

'Does that mean we can cheat as long as we don't get caught?' asked Camilla.

'No it does not.'

'You'd better change the rule then.'

'*I* decide if rules need to be changed,' said

Clive. 'In this case, I happen to agree that rule number one might benefit from some fine tuning. So, I'll start again. Rule number one: No cheating. Rule number two: No cat shall engage in foul play.'

'What's foul play?' asked Tiger.

'Cheating,' said Clive.

'Rule number two is the same as rule number one,' said Camilla. 'We don't need rule number one any more.'

'I'm in charge of the rules!' said Clive. 'But yes, I think you're right, rule number one could be removed.'

'Good,' said Camilla. 'Can we get started now? My muscles are beginning to tighten up.'

'Just a minute,' said Clive. 'If rule number one is to be removed I shall have to renumber rule number two. So, the *new* rule number one is as follows: No foul play, but it is to be changed to no cheating. So, to recap, there is only one rule: No cheating.'

'I'm glad we've sorted that out,' said Douglas.

'It's very important,' said Clive. 'I once knew a cat that was a big cheater.' He laughed.

'Do you get it? A big cheetah!'

The others groaned.

Clive continued. 'The time has come for talking to stop – '

'Hurray,' said Camilla.

'And for competition to start. I am sure you are all eager for action, poised like coiled springs, desperate to stretch yourselves to the limit in the quest to be crowned top cat.'

Clive stared at Bertie, who had nodded off. 'Somebody wake him up, please.'

Douglas gave Bertie a prod.

Bertie opened his eyes. 'Who won?' he said.

'I declare these games open!' shouted Clive.

Bertie got to his feet and yawned. 'I hope this is going to be like the Olympic Games.'

'Does that mean you want to take part in lots of events?' asked Tiger.

'No,' said Bertie. 'I only want them to happen every four years.'

4

Ready... Steady...

'The first event is a sprint,' announced Clive. 'Contestants, please take up your starting positions.'

Camilla and Douglas crouched down ready for action. Tiger jumped up and down on the spot. Bertie sat beside them, motionless.

'You must run the full length of the lawn,' said Clive. 'Touch the fence at the bottom of the garden and return here. Ready… steady… go!'

The four cats raced down the garden. Camilla surged into the lead with Douglas hot on her heels. Tiger and Bertie immediately found themselves in a battle for third place. Camilla was first to reach the fence. She touched it with a paw and doubled back towards the finish. Douglas was nearing her with every stride as Bertie and Tiger fell further and further behind. As Camilla approached the finish line, Douglas managed to catch up with her and get his nose in front to take first place.

'Douglas wins!' shouted Clive.

Tiger and Bertie were still puffing and panting their way home. Tiger was determined not to be last. He managed to produce a final spurt of energy, but in his eagerness to reach the finish line, he tripped and landed in a heap in the middle of the lawn. Bertie staggered home in third place.

'Bad luck, Tiger!' shouted Douglas.

'That was a very dramatic first event,' said Clive. 'I shall now pass you over to my assistant to tell us the scores.'

Tiger got to his feet and shook bits of grass from his fur.

'Four points to Douglas,' he mumbled. 'Three to Camilla, two to Bertie – '

'And none for you,' said Camilla. 'You didn't finish the race.'

'Well done, Douglas,' said Bertie. 'You're the champion. Can we all have a nap now? I'm exhausted.'

'That was only the first event,' said Clive. 'There are two more to go.'

'Good,' said Camilla. 'I'm only just getting warmed up.'

The four contestants followed Clive to the fence at the bottom of the garden.

'The next event is the hurdles,' he said. 'You must take it in turn to run along the top of this fence. As you can see, a number of tree branches are blocking your path and you must jump over them. Whoever completes the course quickest is the winner.'

'I'll go first,' said Douglas.

He scrambled up the fence, crouched into a starting position and waited for Clive to give him the signal.

'Ready… steady… go!'

Douglas worked his way along the top of the fence, stepping over the branches as he went. When he'd cleared the last one he made a quick dash for the finish line.

'Not bad,' said Camilla as she climbed onto the fence. 'Let me show you how it should be done.'

On Clive's signal, Camilla sprang into action. She completed the course within seconds, skipping over the branches as if they weren't there.

'I'd like to see anybody do it faster than that!' she yelled.

'I'm not even going to try,' said Bertie.

'I am,' said Tiger.

Clive gave Tiger the signal to start and the little cat began to walk slowly along the fence. He stopped at the first of the branches before carefully stepping over it. He was about to do

the same with the next one when a light breeze caught it and moved it ever so slightly. Tiger was distracted. He lost his balance, fell off the fence and landed in some weeds.

Camilla laughed. 'No points for you again!'

'Could we please have the scores for that event?' asked Clive.

'Four points to Camilla and three to Douglas,' said Tiger. 'None for me or Bertie,' he added quietly.

'And so to the final event,' said Clive. 'It's called the uphill struggle.'

The others looked at Clive, confused.

'Follow me,' he said with a grin.

Clive led the way to a neighbouring garden and headed for the children's slide in the middle of the lawn. He waited for the others to gather round and then explained what was about to happen.

'All competitors must race *up* the slide and *down* the steps. First to touch the ground is the winner.'

The four cats lined up at the end of the garden and Clive got the final event under way.

Camilla and Douglas were first to reach the slide. The speed of their approach was enough to ensure they could run up the slippery chute. As they reached the top they were neck and neck. Douglas began to pick his way down the wooden steps, but Camilla missed them out and jumped to the ground.

'I win!' she shrieked.

Douglas leaped down after her and ran to Clive.

'I thought we had to run down the steps,' he gasped. 'Camilla missed them out. Is that allowed?'

Camilla charged towards Clive and didn't allow him to answer.

'You said we had to *race* down the steps, not *run* down them,' she said.

Clive thought about it and then gave his decision.

'Camilla wins the uphill struggle!' he announced.

'Yes!' shouted Camilla, punching the air with a paw.

'Perhaps I should have chosen my words more carefully,' said Clive.

'Yes, you should,' said Camilla. 'Words are very important. They have different meanings. I thought you would have known that, Clive.'

Camilla sat down with a smug grin on her face. 'But it's too late now. I'm the winner!'

Meanwhile, Bertie and Tiger were still trying to get up the slide. On their first attempt they'd only managed to get halfway up the chute before losing their footing on the slippery surface. They were back at the bottom in a flash. They tried another run up, but they hadn't built up enough speed and again, they slid back down. On the third attempt Bertie nearly reached the top, but once again his paws gave way beneath him. As he slid down the slide he crashed into Tiger and the two of them were back where they started. This went on for several minutes before Clive finally put a halt to the event.

'And that concludes this exciting athletics contest,' he said. 'Tiger, please tell us the scores for the uphill struggle.'

Tiger couldn't speak because Bertie was sitting on his head. The little cat used what energy he had left to shove his fat friend out of the way and then clambered to his feet.

'Four to Camilla and three to Douglas,' he said.

'Correct,' said Clive. 'And would you please now announce the grand totals.'

'Erm...' Tiger thought for a moment. 'Erm... I'm not quite sure... I've lost count. Sorry.'

'I don't believe it!' said Camilla. 'Not only is he useless at sports, he's useless at adding up too!'

'Don't worry, Tiger,' said Clive. 'I'll work out the final scores and I'll announce them at the closing ceremony, which will take place in Douglas's garden.'

'Why my place?' asked Douglas.

'You can all cool down by having a drink from the pond. Follow me, everybody.'

Clive crawled under the hedge. Camilla was right behind him.

'I won, didn't I?' she asked. 'I'm the champion, aren't I?'

'All will be revealed,' said Clive.

Bertie followed Clive and Camilla. 'I hope we're not going to have to sit through another speech,' he mumbled.

Douglas was about to go after them when he noticed that Tiger was crying.

5

Winners and Losers

Douglas sat down beside Tiger.

'What's wrong?' he asked.

'Camilla's right,' sobbed Tiger. 'I'm useless.'

'You're not useless,' said Douglas.

'Yes I am. I came last in the competition and I couldn't add up the scores!'

'It doesn't matter. You tried your best.'

'It *does* matter! I'm no good at sports and I've got no brains!'

'You're good at other things,' said Douglas.

'No I'm not. I'm no good at anything.'

'*Everybody* is good at something,' said Douglas. '*Everybody* is talented in one way or another.'

'Not me,' said Tiger sadly. 'I'm not talented at all.'

'Of course you are. Talent isn't just about

being good at sports or being brainy, it's about lots of other things too. Sometimes it takes a while for us to realize what our talents are, but I'm sure you'll discover the things you're good at before too long.' Douglas stood up. 'Come on, let's go to the closing ceremony.'

'I don't want to. Camilla will be showing off.'

'She's a good athlete and she won,' said Douglas. 'The least we can do is congratulate her. Come on.'

Clive, Camilla and Bertie were waiting in Douglas's garden. Bertie was gulping water from the small pond. Clive and Camilla were sitting on the lawn.

'Hurry up, you two,' shouted Camilla. 'Clive is about to announce the result.'

Tiger, Douglas and Bertie joined Camilla on the lawn as Clive climbed the three steps onto the patio.

'Congratulations to you all on a most sporting contest,' he said. 'In all competitions there must be a winner – '

'Me,' said Camilla.

'And there must a loser.'

Camilla looked at Tiger and grinned.

'I hereby declare that Camilla, with a total of eleven points, is the Courageous Cats' Club Athletics Champion! I would like to invite her to take her place on the top step.'

Camilla enjoyed every moment as she climbed to the winner's spot.

'Well done, Camilla,' said Douglas.

Camilla raised a paw as a victory salute.

Clive continued. 'In second place, with ten points, was Douglas.'

Clive indicated that Douglas should sit on the second step.

'And in third place with one point,' Clive added, 'was Bertie.'

Bertie was given permission to sit on the bottom step, leaving Tiger alone on the grass.

'Cheer up, Tiger,' said Camilla. 'We'll have another event if you like and I'll give you a chance this time.'

'I think we've had enough for today,' said Douglas. 'We don't have to compete against each other all the time.'

'There's nothing wrong with being competitive,' said Camilla.

'I agree,' said Douglas. 'But we can play games for fun too.'

'You're right,' said Camilla. 'I won the contest so I get to choose the game. Let's play my favourite, chasing birds!'

'I'm not chasing any birds,' said Tiger.

'Why not?' said Camilla. 'Now that you've killed one, I thought you'd have a taste for it.'

'I'm not chasing birds!'

'What do you want to chase then? How about

a squirrel?'

Camilla leaped from the patio and darted down the lawn. She'd spotted a grey squirrel at the end of the garden. The squirrel saw her coming and just managed to make its escape. It scrambled up a wooden post, ran along the top of a fence and shot up a nearby tree. Camilla couldn't be bothered to go after it – she'd spotted another target.

'Anybody want to play Hunt the Hedgehog?'

Camilla crept up to a baby hedgehog rummaging in the leaves at the side of the garden.

'Even you might be able to catch this, Tiger.'

Camilla let out a loud shriek. The tiny hedgehog curled up into a ball, quivering with fear.

Camilla laughed. She walked into the middle of the grass and sat down.

'How about a game of leapfrog, Tiger? All you have to do is this!'

Camilla pounced on a small frog she'd spotted on the lawn and pressed it to the ground beneath her front paws.

'I'm the winner!' she shouted. 'Now let's try for a new world record in the high jump!'

Camilla released the frog which quickly hopped towards the pond. Camilla ran after it.

'You're not getting away that easily,' she said. 'I want to see you jump!'

Camilla poked the frog with one of her paws. The little creature tried to get away by hopping off in another direction. Camilla followed.

'You can do better than that!' she shouted.

Again, she poked the frog. It hopped further down the garden.

'Jump higher!' shouted Camilla.

She jabbed the frog with her claws and laughed as it leaped high into the air. She chased it around the garden, prodding and poking and laughing. Suddenly the frog let out a loud high-pitched scream.

'Leave it alone!' shouted Tiger.

'I'm only playing with it,' said Camilla.

'You're being cruel!'

Camilla took another swipe at the frog. It scrambled under a fence, exhausted.

'I'm going home,' said Tiger.

'Don't be such a baby,' said Camilla.

Tiger scurried into the undergrowth. He hoped the others wouldn't see that he had tears in his eyes.

6

Tiger's Secret

Douglas spotted that Tiger was upset. He jumped from the patio and ran after his friend. He darted into the undergrowth and made his way through the neighbouring gardens as quickly as possible. When he arrived at Tiger's place, he spotted the little cat going into the shed. As Douglas approached, he could hear Tiger talking.

'I'll show her one day. I'll teach Camilla a lesson she'll never forget!'

Douglas poked his head around the shed door. Tiger was sitting on a pile of old sacks. When he saw Douglas, he immediately jumped to his feet.

'Who are you talking to?' asked Douglas.

'Er… nobody,' said Tiger. 'I was talking to myself.'

'I thought only Clive did that.'

Douglas stepped inside and looked around. The shed was very untidy – stacks of dirty plastic plant pots had toppled over and were lying on the floor. Garden tools were scattered around, together with tins of paint, wooden seed trays and various parts of an old lawnmower.

'Why are you sitting in here?' asked Douglas.

'I often do,' said Tiger. 'When I want to be on my own.'

'Do you want to be on your own now? Shall I go?'

'No,' said Tiger. 'But I'm sure you'd prefer to sit in the garden. Come on.'

Tiger ran to the door. Douglas was about to follow when he heard a rustling sound coming from a corner of the shed.

'What was that?' he asked.

'What was what?' said Tiger.

'I heard a noise. It came from behind that old deckchair.'

'It's probably a mouse,' said Tiger. 'It's not doing any harm. Come on, let's go outside.'

'I'm going to take a look.'

Slowly and silently, Douglas began to crawl towards the corner of the shed.

'There's nothing there!' said Tiger urgently.

Douglas peered behind the old chair. He could hardly believe his eyes. Peering back at him was a bird! It had glossy black feathers and a bright yellow beak.

'It's... It's a bird!' Douglas was so shocked, he could barely speak. 'A blackbird!'

'I know,' said Tiger. 'It's the one Camilla caught yesterday.'

'The one you carried into the bushes?'

Tiger nodded.

'But... what's it doing in your shed?'

'He was hurt. I wanted to take care of him, so I brought him here. You won't tell Camilla, will you? She'll laugh at me. I'm supposed to *chase* birds, not look after them.'

'I think what you've done is fantastic,' said Douglas.

'Really?'

'Yes, you've saved his life.'

'I'm not so sure,' said Tiger. 'I think he might die anyway. He hardly ever moves.'

'Perhaps he wants a drink of water,' suggested Douglas.

'I've given him one. I took him to the garden tap. It's always dripping and he stood under it for a while. He drank a little bit, but he still seems unwell.'

'He might want something to eat.'

'I tried to find some food in the bin,' said Tiger. 'But there was nothing.'

'Let me have a look.'

Douglas and Tiger ran to the dustbin, where Douglas examined the contents of the bin bag

that Tiger had ripped open earlier that morning. He picked through the tin cans, yoghurt cartons and squashed plastic bottles, the eggshells, banana skins and used tea bags.

'This will do.' Douglas dragged an apple core from the rubbish. 'Perfect.'

'Birds don't eat apples!' said Tiger. 'Do they?'

'Blackbirds do. They love them.'

'How do you know?'

'I saw it on TV. My owner, Sarah, spends most of her evenings watching the television. Sometimes I sit with her to keep her company. There's a good programme on the Animal Channel every Thursday. It's about birds and animals that live in the garden.'

Tiger picked up the apple core in his mouth and ran to the shed with Douglas. They went inside and Tiger dropped the fruit on the floor. He called out to the bird.

'Here's a present for you, Mr Blackbird.'

The bird didn't move.

'Don't you want it?'

'He'll eat it when he's good and ready,' said Douglas. 'Let's leave him to it.'

The two cats returned to the garden and sat on the grass.

'Do you think he'll be all right?' asked Tiger.

'I'm sure he will.'

'And you won't tell Camilla, will you?'

'Don't worry, your secret is safe with me.'

'There was no need for her to catch that bird,' said Tiger. 'And what she did to the frog and squirrel and hedgehog was rotten. I'm going to teach her a lesson one day.'

'How?' asked Douglas.

'What I'd really like to do is beat her in an athletics contest,' said Tiger. 'I'd love to show her that I'm not useless at sports. That I'm talented like everybody else.' Suddenly, Tiger jumped to his feet. 'I've got an idea!' he said. 'You could be my trainer! You could teach me how to be a great athlete and then I could beat Camilla!'

'I'm not such a great athlete myself,' said Douglas.

'You're better than *me*! Will you do it, Douglas? Will you be my trainer?'

Douglas wasn't sure. 'It would mean a lot of

hard work,' he said.

'It will be worth it!'

Tiger started running round the lawn, taking part in an imaginary race.

'And as they enter the last hundred metres, it's Camilla in the lead,' he shouted. 'But look out, here comes Tiger! Yes, the little ginger cat is closing all the time!' Tiger was running faster and faster, going round and round in circles. 'It's neck and neck!' he shrieked. 'And as they approach the finish line... it's Tiger by a whisker! Tiger is the new sporting champion of the Courageous Cats' Club!'

Tiger collapsed on the grass, panting furiously.

Douglas smiled. 'You'd really like to beat Camilla, wouldn't you?'

'More than anything. Will you help me?'

Douglas nodded. Tiger's right ear began to twitch.

7

Tiger in Training

The first training session took place immediately in Tiger's garden.

'I think we'll start with some running,' said Douglas.

'Good idea,' said Tiger. 'I'll race you to the bottom of the garden.'

'I want to go further than that,' said Douglas. 'Endurance is very important, remember? Let's try running to the bottom of your garden, under the fence and then to the end of old Mr Harding's garden, and all the way back again.'

'OK,' said Tiger. 'Ready… steady…'

'Hang on,' said Douglas. 'I want to show you something.'

Douglas hunched up his body so that all his weight was on his hind legs.

'Your starting position is very important,' he said. 'When the race begins, you must push off with your back feet. Imagine you're a rocket that's just been launched. Like this!'

Douglas sprang forward and shot down the garden. Within seconds, he'd disappeared under the fence. In no time at all, he was on his way back, hurtling towards Tiger.

'As you approach the finish, you must reach out with your nose,' shouted Douglas. 'Use every inch of your body to make sure you cross the winning line first!'

Douglas pelted past Tiger and then slowed to a standstill.

'That was great,' said Tiger as he shuffled into his launch position.

'Don't forget to push off with those hind legs,' said Douglas. 'Ready... steady... go!'

Tiger ran down the garden as fast as his little legs would carry him.

'Go, Tiger, go!' shouted Douglas.

Tiger scrambled under the fence and disappeared. Douglas waited for him to return. He waited... and waited... and waited. Several

minutes passed. Eventually, Tiger crawled under the fence. He was absolutely drenched.

'What happened?' asked Douglas. 'How did you manage to get wet? Mr Harding hasn't got a pond and there are no puddles, because it hasn't rained for days.'

'That's why Mr Harding is watering his lawn,' said Tiger. 'I was halfway across it when the sprinkler came on.' Tiger tried to shake himself dry. 'I hate getting wet!'

'Perhaps we should try something else,' said Douglas. 'Let's have a go at climbing a tree.'

Douglas led the way to the sycamore at the edge of the lawn. Tiger was about to follow when he spotted something moving beneath a pile of leaves.

'Look who's there,' he said. 'It's the baby hedgehog. The one that Camilla frightened.'

He and Douglas went to have a closer look.

'Hello, baby hedgehog,' said Tiger.

The hedgehog quickly curled into a tiny ball and began to tremble.

'He's terrified,' said Tiger. 'Look, he's hiding his face and pointing all his spikes at me.'

'They're not called spikes,' said Douglas. 'They're called spines.'

'How do you know?'

'I learned it from that TV programme. And, for your information, a baby hedgehog is called a hoglet.' Douglas headed back towards the tree. 'Come on,' he said. 'The hoglet isn't going to move while we're standing over him.'

Tiger followed Douglas to the huge sycamore and peered up the towering trunk.

'I'm not very good at climbing trees,' he said.

'Just think of it as more running practice,' said

Douglas. 'But instead of running along the ground, you'll be running up the tree.'

'I'll give it a try.'

Tiger launched himself at the tree trunk and sank his claws into it.

'Now see how high you can go,' said Douglas.

Ever so slowly, Tiger worked his way up. At this moment, the grey squirrel was making his way down. Halfway up the tree, Tiger and the squirrel came face to face. They both let out a

shriek. The squirrel turned round and zipped to the highest branch. Tiger lost his footing and fell to the ground.

'Arrrrgghhhh!'

He managed to land on his feet and was more surprised than hurt.

'That squirrel gave me a fright!' said Tiger.

'I think you gave him a fright too,' said Douglas.

Tiger looked up into the tree and spotted the squirrel peering down nervously.

'Sorry I scared you, Mr Squirrel!'

'He probably thought you were going to chase him, just like Camilla did,' said Douglas.

Tiger called out again. 'Don't worry, Mr Squirrel. I'm going to teach her a lesson!'

Douglas wandered down the garden and hopped onto an upturned bucket.

'Let's try some jumping,' he said. 'Once again, your starting position is crucial.' Douglas made his whole body as small as possible. 'Again, you need to push off with your back legs.'

Douglas leaped gracefully through the air and landed on a wall a couple of metres away.

'Good jump!' said Tiger. 'Let me have a go.'

Tiger climbed onto the bucket and steadied himself. He scrunched up into a little ball and then pushed off. Douglas closed his eyes as Tiger crashed into the wall, slid down it and landed in some nettles.

'Owww!'

'I think that's enough training for today,' said Douglas.

Tiger carefully picked his way back to the lawn and sat down. He was surprised to find himself sitting next to the frog.

'Hello, Froggy. What are you doing here?'

The little cat had never seen a frog close up. He carefully studied its smooth green skin speckled with dark blotches.

'Why don't you go back to your pond?' asked Tiger. 'Are you lost? Would you like me to show you the way?'

Tiger gave the frog a gentle push. The frog let out a cry of distress.

'It's OK,' said Tiger. 'I'm not going to hurt you.'

Once more, Tiger tried to encourage the frog to move, but again, it let out a scream.

'I think you'd better leave him alone,' said Douglas.

'Every creature I've met today has been terrified of me,' said Tiger. 'They all think I want to hurt them because of what Camilla did. I'm fed up with it!'

Tiger stormed off down the garden.

'Where are you going?' shouted Douglas.

'To challenge Camilla to a sporting contest!'

'What about the training?'

'We've finished, haven't we?'

Douglas chased after Tiger. 'We've only just started! It could take weeks! Perhaps months!'

Tiger wasn't listening. His mind was made up. He was going to challenge Camilla right away.

8

The Challenge

Tiger marched through the gardens. Douglas was in hot pursuit, protesting every step of the way.

'It's too soon!' he shouted. 'You're not ready to compete against her!'

Tiger took no notice. He was determined to issue the challenge and he wanted everybody to hear it.

He called at Clive's and found the big old cat sitting on the step at the back of his house.

'What's going on?' asked Clive.

'I'm on my way to Camilla's,' said Tiger. 'I think you'll want to hear what I've got to say to her.'

Clive immediately followed Tiger and Douglas to Bertie's place.

Tiger jumped onto the window sill and looked into Bertie's kitchen. Bertie was snoozing in his basket. Tiger tapped on the window with a paw and Bertie opened his eyes. After a moment, he got to his feet, walked round in a circle on his blanket, lay down again and went back to sleep. Tiger dropped to the ground and clambered through the cat flap. He checked that Bertie's owners weren't around and then woke him up.

'What's going on?' said Bertie.

'I'm going to see Camilla. Clive and Douglas are coming with me and I think you should come too.'

Bertie climbed out of his bed, wandered over to his bowl and swallowed a mouthful of cat food.

'This had better be important,' he said.

Tiger jumped through the cat flap and Bertie squeezed through after him.

The cats made their way to Camilla's. She was sunbathing in the middle of the lawn and was woken by the sound of the four visitors crawling under the hedge.

'What's going on?' she asked.

'I challenge you to a sporting contest!' said Tiger.

Camilla burst out laughing. 'Is this a joke?'

'It's not a very funny one,' said Bertie. 'I've been dragged from my bed for this nonsense.'

'It's not nonsense,' said Tiger. 'I'm challenging Camilla.'

'It's too soon,' said Douglas. 'You need more

training.'

'Training?' Camilla laughed again. 'This sounds serious.'

'It is serious!' said Tiger.

'And when is this sporting contest going to take place?' asked Camilla.

'Tomorrow.'

'You won't be ready by then,' said Douglas.

'I'll be ready,' insisted Tiger.

Clive sighed. 'I suppose you're going to want me to organize it,' he said.

'No thanks,' said Tiger. 'I'm going to do it, but I would like some help. Would you be the official race starter, please?'

'Very well,' said Clive.

Tiger turned to Bertie. 'And I'd like you to be the scorekeeper, please.'

'A very good choice,' said Bertie. 'The job requires great intelligence, with which I happen to be blessed.'

'What about the rules?' asked Clive.

'There's only one rule,' said Tiger. 'No cruelty to animals.'

Clive, Camilla, Bertie and Douglas were

puzzled.

'What are you talking about?' said Camilla.

'What you did to that blackbird and frog and squirrel and hedgehog was horrible and you're not doing it again,' said Tiger.

'Baby!' sneered Camilla.

'The contest will take place in my garden at ten o'clock tomorrow,' said Tiger. 'If any other animals are there you have to leave them alone. Agreed?'

'OK,' said Camilla. 'I'll agree to your rule if you'll agree to *my* rule.'

'What rule is that?' asked Tiger.

'The loser of the contest has to jump into the pond!'

'I don't understand.'

'Whoever loses the sporting contest has to jump into the pond in Douglas's garden. It will make things more interesting.'

'That's silly.'

'Are you frightened of losing?'

'No,' said Tiger. 'I've got talents like everybody else and I'm going to prove it!'

'In that case, I'm sure you'll agree to my rule,'

said Camilla, with a grin. 'The loser has to jump
into the pond.'

'OK,' said Tiger.

Bertie shook his head in disbelief. 'This is
madness.'

'Are you sure you know what you're doing,
Tiger?' asked Douglas.

'I'm sure.'

Tiger strode down the garden trying to look
confident. Inside he could feel his heart thumping
like never before.

9

Visiting Time

Tiger crawled under the hedge into his garden. Douglas followed.

'You'll never be ready for tomorrow,' said Douglas urgently.

'I'll start training right away,' said Tiger.

'There isn't enough time!'

'We've got all afternoon. We'll do some more running practice and then – '

Tiger stopped speaking and pricked up his ears. A cheeping sound was coming from the shed.

'Can you hear that?' he whispered.

Douglas nodded. 'It must be the blackbird.'

The two cats crept towards the shed. As they did so, the cheeping was replaced by a squeaking and then a humming.

'I never realized blackbirds made so many

different noises,' said Tiger quietly.

The two cats popped their heads around the door. The blackbird was perched on an upturned plant pot. When it saw the two cats, it hopped onto the floor and scurried behind the deckchair.

'Look!' said Tiger. 'He's eaten the apple!'

Douglas and Tiger stepped inside and examined what was left of the fruit – a stalk and a couple of pips.

'Did you enjoy your snack, Mr Blackbird?' said Tiger.

The blackbird peered out from his hiding place and gave a little nod followed by a shrill whistle.

'Shall I try and find you another one?'

The blackbird nodded again and Tiger dashed into the garden. Douglas ran after him.

'Tiger, I want to have a word with you about tomorrow's contest.'

Tiger wasn't listening. His mind was on other things. 'I think I'll go and visit the hoglet and the squirrel and the frog,' he said, 'to see if they're all right.'

'But I want to talk to you about the training,'

said Douglas.

'We'll start training soon. Come on.'

Tiger ran to the pile of leaves where he'd last seen the hoglet.

'He's still here!' he shouted. 'Come and see!'

The hoglet quickly curled into a little ball as Douglas approached.

'Do you think he's OK?' asked Tiger.

'I don't know,' said Douglas.

'Perhaps he's hungry. What do hoglets eat?'

'I once saw a fully grown hedgehog eating out of a dog's bowl,' said Douglas.

Tiger laughed. 'Really? Where was that?'

'On TV.'

'Of course. I forgot you spend most of your time watching telly.'

Douglas smiled.

'Perhaps the hoglet would like some cat food,' said Tiger.

The little cat hurried towards his house, nipped through the cat flap and reappeared a moment later with a chunk of cat food in his mouth. He dropped the meat on the ground and stepped back. Ever so slowly, the hoglet

uncurled itself and sniffed the air with its little
snout. Then it scurried to the cat meat and
gobbled it up.

'He loves it!' said Tiger.

'Good,' said Douglas. 'Now can we talk about
the training? I've given it some thought and – '

Douglas was interrupted by a little squeak
from the hoglet.

'What's the matter, hoglet?' asked Tiger.

The hoglet jerked sharply.

'Are you all right?'

Suddenly the hoglet was squeaking and
jerking uncontrollably.

'Oh no!' said Tiger. He turned to Douglas.

'What shall we do?'

'There's nothing we can do.'

'What do you mean?' said Tiger. 'What's wrong with him?'

'He's eaten the cat meat too quickly. He's got the hiccups!'

Douglas and Tiger laughed as the hoglet continued to squeak and jerk.

'I think I'll call him Hiccup from now on,' said Tiger. 'Hiccup the hoglet!'

'That's a great name,' said Douglas.

'Come on,' said Tiger. 'Let's go and see how Froggy is getting on.'

The frog was still sitting on the lawn. It had barely moved since Tiger saw it last.

'Are you still here?' said Tiger. 'It's very hot to be out in the open. It's not very safe either. If Camilla comes along she might decide to have another game of leapfrog.'

Tiger reached out a paw and gave the frog a little nudge. The frog let out a scream.

'It's OK,' said Tiger. 'I'm your friend, remember? I can show you a nice cool place where you'll be safe. Would you like that?'

For a moment, the frog was silent and still. Then it gave a deep throaty croak followed by a sharp nod of its head.

Tiger gave the frog another gentle push and it moved ever so slightly. The little cat carefully encouraged the frog to take one small hop after another and they gradually worked their way to

the bottom of the garden.

'Where are you taking him?' asked Douglas.

'You'll see.'

Tiger guided the frog under the fence into Mr Harding's garden. Douglas followed.

'Nearly there,' said Tiger as he eased the frog towards the plants at the edge of the lawn.

'It's nice and damp here, Froggy. I should know, I got soaked earlier!'

The frog hopped under a huge leaf and settled down on the moist soil.

'If you stay here, you should be fine,' said Tiger. 'The sprinkler might even come on again and you'll get a nice shower. I'll call by and see you again later. Goodbye, Froggy.'

Tiger headed back towards his garden.

'Come on Douglas, I'm going to practise my tree climbing.'

Douglas was amazed. 'Do you mean you're finally going to do some training?'

'No,' said Tiger. 'I'm going to look for the squirrel!'

10

Talented Tiger

Tiger peered up into the sycamore tree. High above his head, the grey squirrel was flitting nimbly from branch to branch. The two cats watched as the squirrel worked its way down the tree, gripping the branches with its claws and using its long bushy tail for balance. The squirrel stopped above a wooden bird feeder that was hanging by a piece of string from one of the branches. The feeder was shaped like a little house. A door and two tiny windows were covered with wire mesh, through which birds could peck at the peanuts inside.

'He's after those nuts!' said Tiger. 'Look!'

The squirrel eased itself onto the top of the feeder and scratched at the wire.

'He can't get at them,' said Douglas.

The squirrel pressed its face against one of the little windows. Still it couldn't reach the food inside.

'He needs some help,' said Tiger.

As quick as a flash, the little cat hurled himself at the tree trunk and began to climb. The squirrel immediately abandoned the house and darted to the top of the tree.

'Don't worry, Mr Squirrel,' shouted Tiger. 'I'm going to help you.'

'How are you going to do that?' asked Douglas.

'I'm not sure yet.'

Tiger worked his way higher and higher, the squirrel watching his every move.

'You won't be able to pull the peanuts out through the wire,' shouted Douglas. 'Besides, they're meant for birds, not squirrels.'

'The birds don't bother with them in the summer,' shouted Tiger. 'I'm sure they won't mind if Mr Squirrel has them.'

Tiger was now halfway up the tree. He inched his way carefully along a branch until he was above the bird feeder. He crouched down, stretched out a paw and placed it on the roof of

the little house. It swayed from side to side.

'Be careful!' shouted Douglas.

Tiger now had both his front paws pressed against the house. He pushed down as hard as he could. Suddenly, the string snapped. Tiger just managed to keep his balance and remain on the branch as the bird feeder fell to the ground. It exploded on impact and peanuts flew in every direction. Before Tiger could move, the squirrel zipped down the trunk and grabbed one of the nuts between its front claws.

'You'll enjoy those nuts, won't you, Mr Squirrel?' shouted Tiger.

The squirrel nodded, popped the nut into its mouth and shot back to the top of the tree.

Tiger shuffled down the trunk and dropped to the ground.

'Enjoy your snack, Mr Squirrel!' he yelled. 'There's plenty more down here!' Tiger inspected the peanuts. 'I wonder if the blackbird would like one of these. What do you think, Douglas?'

'I think you and I should have a talk.'

'A talk about what?' asked Tiger.

'Tomorrow's sporting contest. You against Camilla. I think you should call it off.'

Tiger was stunned. 'What? Why?'

'When I agreed to be your trainer, I thought you were going to put in a lot of hard work. It's obvious you'd rather spend your time looking after these animals.'

Tiger didn't say anything so Douglas continued.

'Challenging Camilla to a sporting contest is a brave thing to do, but insisting the contest takes place tomorrow is crazy. Camilla is a very good athlete.'

'You don't think I can beat her, do you?' said Tiger quietly. 'You don't think I'm talented.'

'I think you're *very* talented,' said Douglas. 'You've already proved that by helping the blackbird and the squirrel and the frog and the hoglet.'

Tiger didn't understand. 'What do you mean?'

'Talent isn't just about being good at sports or being brainy, it's about lots of other things too. Helping others is a talent.'

'Is it?'

'Of course it is,' said Douglas. 'Not everybody knows how to do it. And those that do know how to do it don't always bother. Sometimes we get so wrapped up in ourselves, we don't notice that others might need a bit of help.'

'I've never thought about it like that before,' said Tiger. He smiled. 'So I *am* talented!'

'Everybody is talented,' said Douglas. 'But we have to remember that we're all good at different things.'

Tiger sighed. 'And I suppose I'm not really very good at sports.'

'One day you might be, but I don't think you're going to turn into a super athlete over night. That's why I think you should call off the contest.'

'But I really want to beat Camilla,' said Tiger.

'I think you'll have to save that for another day. Let's go and see her now and tell her you want to withdraw your challenge.'

'Not now,' said Tiger. 'I'll tell her tomorrow. Right now I want to try and find another snack for the blackbird.'

Tiger ran down the garden. Suddenly he stopped and turned to Douglas.

'Thanks for being a great trainer!' he shouted.

'I haven't done anything,' said Douglas.

'Yes you have. You've made me realize that I'm talented!'

Tiger disappeared beneath the fence.

11

A Shock for Camilla

The next morning, Douglas called at Tiger's house and found him sitting beneath the sycamore tree. He wasn't alone. The grey squirrel was hopping around beside him.

'Has he eaten all the peanuts?' asked Douglas.

'He's eaten some of them,' said Tiger. 'He's buried the rest. I've been watching him. He digs a little hole, drops in a nut and then pats down the earth on top of it. I guess he'll sniff them out again when he wants them.'

'How are your other patients?' asked Douglas.

'They're fine,' said Tiger. 'I went to check on them earlier. It took me a while to find Froggy. He'd changed colour to blend in with the surroundings.'

'I didn't know frogs could do that,' said Douglas.

'Neither did I. And I didn't know that hedgehogs are good climbers until I saw Hiccup the hoglet scrambling up a fence! The more I watch the other animals, the more I learn about them.'

'What about the blackbird?' asked Douglas. 'Is he still in the shed?'

'No, he's flown away, but I'm hoping he'll come back later.'

'You've done a great job looking after them,' said Douglas. 'Helping others is definitely one of your talents.'

Tiger wandered towards his house with Douglas by his side.

'I've been thinking about everything we talked about yesterday,' said Tiger. 'And you're right. I'm not very good at running, climbing or jumping. If I compete against Camilla, I'll almost certainly lose.'

At this moment Camilla, Clive and Bertie scrambled under the hedge.

'Make way for the champion!' shouted Camilla.

The squirrel immediately darted behind the

tree trunk and hid.

Tiger jumped onto the garden bench. 'Gather round, everybody,' he said. 'I have something to say.'

'I hope you're not going to make a speech,' said Bertie.

'As you know, I have challenged Camilla to a sporting contest. Before we get started I'd like to remind everybody of the rules.'

Douglas was confused. 'I thought you were going to call off the contest,' he said.

'No way,' said Tiger. 'Rule number one: No cruelty to animals. Rule number two: The loser has to jump into the pond.'

'I hope you've been practising your swimming,' said Camilla.

Tiger ignored her. 'Follow me, everybody, and we'll get started.'

'Are you sure you want to go through with this, Tiger?' asked Douglas.

'I'm sure.'

Tiger led the cats down the garden towards the sycamore where Camilla spotted the grey squirrel hiding behind the trunk.

'What's *he* doing here? He'd better clear off if he knows what's good for him.'

'Leave him alone,' said Tiger. 'If you harm him, you'll have broken a rule and I'll be the winner of the contest.'

'What is the first event?' asked Clive.

'A race to the top of the tree,' said Tiger.

Clive cleared his throat and spoke with his official race-starter's voice. 'Competitors, please take up your positions.'

Camilla crouched down, ready to launch herself at the tree trunk. Tiger didn't move.

'Are you ready, Tiger?' asked Clive. 'I'm about to start the race.'

'I'm not taking part,' said Tiger.

'That makes me the winner!' shouted Camilla.

'Do you want to call off the contest, Tiger?' asked Douglas.

'No.'

Clive was baffled. 'But you just said you're not going to take part.'

'I'm not,' said Tiger. He raised a paw and pointed it at the squirrel. '*He* is.'

'What are you talking about?' said Camilla.

'I'm supposed to be racing against *you*. It was *you* that challenged me.'

'That's right,' said Tiger. 'But I didn't actually say I would be taking part. I've asked the squirrel to take my place.'

'That's not allowed!' protested Camilla. 'If you don't take part, I'm the winner!'

Clive shook his head. 'I'm afraid not,' he said. 'Tiger said he wanted to *challenge* you, he didn't say he wanted to *compete* against you. Words are very important. They have different meanings. I thought you would have known that, Camilla.'

'So you have to race against the squirrel,' said Tiger. 'Or I'm the winner.'

'Fine!' said Camilla. 'I can beat anybody!'

Once again, Camilla crouched down ready for action. Instantly, the squirrel lay flat on the ground, its long tail twitching furiously.

'Ready...' said Clive. 'Steady... go!'

Camilla threw herself at the tree trunk and scrambled up it as fast as she could. Within a matter of seconds, she'd reached the highest branch. To her horror, the squirrel was sitting there waiting for her.

'No!' she screamed. 'That's not possible!'

'One point to the squirrel,' shouted Bertie. 'Or perhaps I should say one point to Tiger!'

Camilla scuttled down the tree and ran to Clive. 'There must be more than one squirrel,' she said. 'It's a trick. One of them was hiding in the tree and – '

'The squirrel won the race,' said Clive. 'I saw it with my own eyes. Believe me, he's fast.'

As if to prove it, the squirrel ran down the tree as quickly as it had run up. It sat down beside Tiger.

'Well done,' said the little cat. 'And thanks.'

'What's the next event?' asked Clive.

'The long jump,' said Tiger. 'Whoever jumps furthest down the garden path is the winner. Another of my friends will be entering this event.'

At this moment the blackbird fluttered down onto the lawn.

'Hello,' said Tiger. 'So glad you could make it.' He turned to Camilla. 'This is the blackbird you caught the other day. As you can see, he's now fully recovered.'

'I don't care,' said Camilla. 'It won't be able to beat me. Everybody knows birds can't jump!'

Camilla wandered to the end of the path. She hardly put in any effort at all as she made a short jump. She glared at the blackbird.

'I'd like to see you beat that!'

'The blackbird isn't competing in this event,' said Tiger.

'You said it was!' shouted Camilla.

'No I didn't. I said another of my friends would be competing. I didn't say which one.'

Just then, the frog hopped across the lawn and sat at the end of the path.

'Froggy will be taking part in the long jump,' said Tiger.

'Wait a minute!' said Camilla. 'I want another go! I didn't know that – '

'You've had your turn,' said Clive. 'Let's see what the next competitor can do.'

The frog leaped high into the air and landed halfway down the path.

'Another point to Tiger!' shouted Bertie.

'No!' screamed Camilla. 'It's not fair!'

'Tiger hasn't broken any rules,' said Clive.

'And now for the final event,' said Tiger. 'I've placed a piece of bacon rind at the bottom of old Mr Harding's garden. The first competitor to reach it and bring it here is the winner.' Tiger smiled at Camilla. 'It's you against the blackbird this time.'

'Ready...' said Clive. 'Steady... go!'

'What's the point?' muttered Camilla.

She lay on the ground and watched as the blackbird took off and flew down the garden. It glided over the fence and disappeared from view. In no time at all it was back with the bacon in its beak.

'Well done,' said Tiger. 'You can have the bacon as a prize.'

The blackbird dropped the bacon on the ground and pecked at it gratefully.

'Another point to Tiger!' shouted Bertie. 'That makes the final score Tiger three, Camilla zero!'

'What a result!' said Clive. 'The contest wasn't quite what we were expecting, but Tiger is definitely the winner.'

'Me and my animal friends,' said Tiger.

'Congratulations!' said Douglas.

'Bravo!' added Bertie. 'It was really smart of you to outwit Camilla like that.'

'I'm simply bursting with talent,' laughed Tiger.

'All right, all right,' said Camilla. 'You've had your fun, but it's over now.'

'Not quite,' said Clive. 'Tiger is the winner, which makes you the loser. That means you have to jump into the pond.'

A look of terror crept over Camilla's face. 'But… but...'

Clive ran across the lawn and scrambled under the fence.

'Come on, everybody,' he shouted. 'Let's go to Douglas's garden!'

'Wait!' said Camilla, chasing after Clive. 'Wait! We need to talk about this!'

Bertie ran after them. 'I wouldn't miss this for anything,' he chuckled.

Douglas strolled over to Tiger. 'Well done!'

'Thanks,' said Tiger. 'I was determined to find a way to beat Camilla and the other animals were only too pleased to help.'

'And they can hardly wait to see her jump into the pond,' said Douglas. 'Look!'

The squirrel, frog and blackbird were scrabbling under the fence. They couldn't get to Douglas's garden fast enough.

12

Will She or Won't She?

The animals filed into Douglas's garden and gathered round the pond. Camilla stared into the water.

'It was a joke,' she said feebly. 'When I said the loser had to jump into the pond, I didn't mean it.'

'You made the rule,' said Tiger.

'That's right,' said Clive. 'In you go.'

Camilla began to panic. 'You don't seriously expect me to jump into the water?'

She looked at each of the cats in turn. They all nodded.

'You don't really expect me to mess up my beautiful coat?'

The cats nodded again.

'It would be cruel,' said Camilla. Suddenly her face lit up. 'Yes! It would be cruel! And rule number one clearly states no cruelty to animals!' She turned to Tiger. 'I'm right, aren't I?'

Tiger didn't know what to say.

Camilla looked eagerly at Clive. 'I'm right, aren't I? You're an expert on rules, aren't you, Clive? One of the rules was no cruelty to animals, wasn't it?'

Clive thought about it. 'You do have a point.'

'If Tiger forces me to jump into the water, it would be cruel!'

'You were cruel to the blackbird,' said Tiger. 'And the squirrel and – '

'I was just playing with them.'

'You were cruel to them!'

'How about I apologize?' suggested Camilla desperately. 'Then you could let me off, couldn't you, Tiger?'

Camilla didn't wait for an answer. She turned to the frog. 'I'm sorry I prodded and poked you.' Then to the squirrel. 'I'm sorry I chased you out of the garden. And I'm sorry to you too, blackbird. There was no need for me to pick on you like that.' Camilla looked at Tiger. 'There, I've said I'm sorry. I've apologized to every creature I tormented. Please don't make me jump into the pond.'

'I think you owe Tiger an apology as well,' said Douglas. 'You picked on him because he didn't want to chase birds. That's what started all of this.'

'You're right,' said Camilla. 'I'm sorry, Tiger. Please forgive me. You don't have to chase birds if you don't want to. We're still friends, aren't we?'

Tiger nodded.

'And you wouldn't force a friend to jump into the pond, would you?'

Tiger thought about it.

'Please, Tiger,' said Camilla. 'I've said I'm sorry to all those I harmed. I don't have to jump in, do I?'

Tiger shook his head. 'No,' he said quietly.

Camilla gave a huge sigh of relief and sat down. Unfortunately for her, she'd sat on Hiccup the hoglet. He'd been listening to all of this and wasn't amused when he was left out of the apologies. Ever so quietly he'd sneaked up behind Camilla and curled himself into a little ball, exposing hundreds of tiny sharp spines. There was a slight pause before Camilla let out a terrific scream.

'Yeeooowww!'

She shot high into the air. A few seconds later, she landed in the pond with a terrific splash. There was another pause before Camilla leaped out of the water and started running round the garden, screaming.

'Look at me! I'm soaked! Look at my beautiful coat!'

Clive, Bertie, Tiger and Douglas laughed. The squirrel, the frog and the blackbird hopped up and down with glee.

'Cheer up, Camilla,' shouted Tiger. 'I think you just set a new world record for the high jump!'

Everybody laughed.

Stars in Their Eyes

Contents

1

⠿

Emergency

Sarah placed her cup of tea on the coffee table and settled into her armchair.

'We've been looking forward to this all week, haven't we?' she said.

Douglas answered with a loud miaow. He jumped into Sarah's lap and curled up, ready to watch TV.

'Welcome to the Isle of Man,' said the lady on the television. 'This tiny island in the middle of the Irish Sea is well known for its beautiful scenery, its annual motorbike races and, of course, its cats!'

Sarah tickled Douglas under his chin and he began to purr contentedly.

'Cats from this island are known as Manx cats,' said the lady. 'They're quite unlike any other. Do you know why that is?'

'Because they don't have a tail!' said Sarah.

'Because they don't have a tail!' agreed the lady.

'And they're very, very cute,' said Sarah. 'Just like my Douglas.'

'Later in the programme we'll be meeting some Manx cats, but before that we'll take a quick tour around the island.'

That's when Douglas heard the high-pitched yowl coming from a nearby garden. He stopped purring, pricked up his ears and listened carefully. There it was again! To the human ear it sounded like any other cat noise and Sarah hardly noticed it, but to Douglas it was no ordinary sound. It meant only one thing – an emergency!

Douglas jumped to the floor, ran across the room and rested his front paws on the TV cabinet.

'Oh, well done, Douglas,' said Sarah. 'I forgot to switch on the DVD – thanks for reminding me.'

Sarah reached for the remote control and pressed the record button.

'We'll want to watch this programme again

and again, won't we?'

Douglas didn't answer. He'd already left the house through an open window.

Clive was playing golf when he heard it. He'd found a ball in the weeds at the bottom of his garden and was flicking it with one of his paws towards a hole in the lawn. He was delighted somebody was making the emergency call – it meant the possibility of action and adventure. He instantly abandoned his game and scrambled under the fence.

Camilla was sitting on her lawn having a wash. She'd spent almost an hour grooming herself and was feeling particularly pleased with her appearance. The last thing she wanted was an emergency – she'd been looking forward to a spot of sunbathing, but that would have to wait now. She got to her feet and ran down the garden.

Bertie was asleep in his basket. He was having a bad dream – somebody was stealing his lunch! He twitched and moaned and tossed and turned until the yowling woke him up. He immediately ran to his bowl and was relieved to see his food was still there. He quickly gobbled a mouthful of fishy chunks – he couldn't face an emergency on an empty stomach. Then he squeezed through his cat flap and headed for the apple tree at the bottom of his garden.

That's where the others were heading, too – all eager to find out why one of the gang wanted to hold an emergency meeting of the Courageous Cats' Club!

2

Wanted!

Tiger had never called an emergency meeting before. He felt very important when he saw Douglas, Clive, Camilla and Bertie charging towards him.

'What's wrong, Tiger?' shouted Clive.

'What's happened?' yelled Camilla urgently.

The four cats joined Tiger beneath the apple tree.

'I hope this is important,' gasped Bertie.

'What's the emergency?' asked Douglas.

'They want an ordinary cat!' said Tiger excitedly, his right ear twitching quickly. 'I saw it in the newspaper. About the television company. It could be one of us!'

He was making no sense at all.

'Take your time,' said Clive.

Tiger stood up to reveal the scrap of newspaper on which he'd been sitting.

'I saw this. I managed to rip it out. I thought you'd want to see it.'

Douglas placed a paw on the piece of paper to stop it from blowing away and began to read.

'Wanted: a cat with purr-sonality! The search is on for a cat to be the star of a brand new television programme, *Paws for Thought*. The chosen moggy will be filmed in its home every day for a week.'

'That's not an emergency!' said Bertie.

'Shhh!' said the others.

Douglas continued to read. ' "We want to record the everyday life of an ordinary cat," said Julian Jones of the Animal Channel. "We want to explore the mind and habits of this fascinating creature. We will, of course, pay a fee to the cat's owner." '

Bertie wasn't impressed. 'Have I been forced from my bed because of a titbit in the local newspaper? The emergency signal is only to be sounded for very serious matters!'

'This *is* serious,' said Camilla. 'It's my chance

to become a TV star.' She licked a paw and dabbed her face. 'I'll look as beautiful on television as I do in real life.'

'*I'm* the one they'll choose,' said Tiger. 'I'm young and talented!'

'They might want a Manx cat,' said Douglas. 'There aren't many of us round here.'

'If they're looking for a cat without a tail you'll have to compete against me,' said Clive. 'And I know who will win.'

'Excuse me,' said Bertie. 'When you've all finished fantasizing, could somebody please remind me about the rule regarding emergencies!'

Clive was happy to oblige. 'The rule states that if anybody sounds the emergency signal in a situation which is *not* an emergency, they will be thrown out of the club.'

Tiger was suddenly very worried. 'I thought… I didn't mean to…'

'It's all right,' said Clive. 'You thought it was an emergency and so you did the right thing. In future, however, we need to decide precisely what counts as an emergency.'

'An emergency is a matter of life or death,' said Bertie.

Clive considered Bertie's suggestion. 'Very well,' he said eventually. 'From now on the rule is as follows: If anybody sounds the emergency signal in a situation which is *not* a matter of life or death, they will be thrown out of the club. And I'd just like to remind everybody that failure to attend an emergency meeting will also result in the offending cat being thrown out.'

'Yes, yes, yes,' said Camilla. 'Now can we get back to the television programme? I happen to think it's important. I've always dreamed of being famous.'

'Me too,' said Tiger. 'When I've appeared in this programme, I'll be so famous that I'll be asked to appear in television adverts for cat food!'

'Do you think that's possible?' asked Bertie, who was suddenly very interested.

'Anything's possible in show business,' said Tiger.

'And how would one go about trying to appear in this programme?'

Douglas had another look at the newspaper article.

'Anybody interested should take their cat along to the town hall at two o'clock on Sunday.'

'That's today!' said Camilla.

'I know,' said Tiger. 'I told you it was an emergency.'

Camilla began to panic. 'My owners can't take me, they've gone out.'

'Mine too,' said Clive.

'We could go by ourselves,' said Bertie.

'They won't let us take part if we don't have our owner with us,' said Tiger.

'We don't know that,' argued Camilla.

'Let's vote on it,' said Clive. 'All those in favour of trying out for the television programme, raise a paw.'

Clive was the only one to vote. The others were already halfway down the garden on their way to the town hall.

3

Smile Please

Clive was last to leave the garden, but first to arrive at the town hall. He wasn't usually a fast runner, but he'd raced past the others in an effort to be first on the scene.

Tiger and Douglas were next. They'd calmly trotted along side by side, the young cat quizzing his friend on how to go about securing his big break in TV.

'You need to make an impression,' said Douglas.

'What does that mean?' asked Tiger.

'Get yourself noticed.'

Bertie had run as fast as he could, spurred on by the thought of spending all day eating cat food in a TV commercial. When he reached the town hall he collapsed on the pavement, exhausted.

Last to arrive was Camilla. She'd walked all the way so she wouldn't get too hot – she wanted to look her best for the cameras.

The five cats stared at the long line of people queuing up to get into the building. Each of them was holding a cat. There were big cats, small cats, thin cats, fat cats, noisy cats and quiet cats.

'I didn't realize anybody else would be here,' said Tiger.

Clive laughed. 'You're not the only one who wants to be on TV,' he said.

A bald man was trying to organize the proceedings. 'Take a ticket with a number on it,' he shouted to the people in the queue. 'When you're inside, wait for your number to be called and one of our photographers will take a shot of your cat.'

'A shot?' said Tiger, with a worried look on his face.

'A photograph,' said Camilla.

'Please be patient,' shouted the bald man. 'Everybody will be seen.'

'We won't be able to get tickets,' said Tiger.

'We'll just have to manage without,' said Clive. 'Are we going to push in?'

'The humans won't mind, they love queuing.'

The five cats wove their way through a maze of human legs towards the big wooden doors of the town hall. Once inside, they followed the cardboard arrows fastened to the walls and found themselves in the mayor's lounge. They scurried beneath a grand piano where they sat down and looked around the room. Huge paintings of important people hung on the walls. Thick red curtains were draped around the windows. Sparkling chandeliers dangled from the ceiling. At the end of the room was a large stage, in the centre of which was a sculpture of a man's head and shoulders.

'Look at that statue!' said Tiger. 'Is it the mayor?'

'Probably,' said Bertie. 'But it's not a statue, it's a bust.'

'A bust?'

'Yes. A sculpture of a person's head and shoulders is called a bust.'

There were lots of people in the room and

nearly as many cats. A lady with a clipboard was calling out numbers and pointing the cat owners towards one or the other of the two photographers who had set up their equipment in a corner of the room. One of them was an old man with a camera on a tripod. He was carefully lining up a shot of a Siamese cat sitting on a table. The other, a young lady with a camera round her neck, was snapping away furiously at a kitten lying on the shiny wooden floor. Another photographer was wandering around casually taking pictures of various cats as they waited their turns.

'How can we get ourselves noticed?' asked Tiger.

'Like this!' said Clive.

He ran across the room and darted up one of the thick curtains. When he'd reached the top he let out a loud miaow.

'Look at that cat!' somebody shouted.

The young lady photographer ran towards the curtain and began taking pictures of Clive.

'He hasn't got a tail!' she said.

The old photographer quickly lifted his

camera from the tripod and moved closer so
that he too could get a picture of Clive.

'Perhaps he's a Manx cat,' he said.

Douglas wasn't amused. *He's not a Manx cat,* he
thought. *But I am!*

Douglas ran towards the young photographer
and rubbed against her leg.

'Here's another one!' she said.

The two photographers took a few snaps of Douglas.

Clive was furious that he was no longer the centre of attention. He let out a loud shriek and began to slide slowly down the curtain, ripping the luxurious material with his sharp claws. Now all eyes were back on him.

Camilla meanwhile had climbed onto the bust of the mayor at the front of the stage. She let out a long loud wail. Everybody turned to look at her. Camilla draped herself over the mayor's head, one paw over his face like an eyepatch. The photographers ran towards her, clicking furiously. Camilla sat up and flashed her teeth at the cameras. Then she lay down and rolled onto her back. The bust toppled forward. Everybody gasped. Camilla leaped clear as the bust fell from the stage and shattered into hundreds of pieces on the floor.

Douglas rushed over to Tiger. 'Now you know why it's called a bust,' he said.

Tiger nodded. 'Because it's bust!'

'Come on,' said Douglas. 'I think we'd better

get out of here.'

'But I haven't had my picture taken!' said
Tiger.

The little cat ran across the room. As he
approached the photographers he tried to stop,
but the shiny wooden floor was very slippery.
He slid past the photographers and crashed into
the tripod. It fell over and just missed the
Siamese cat sitting on the table.

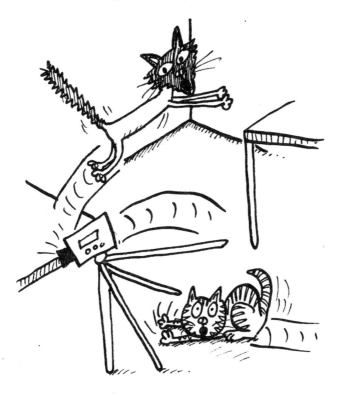

All the noise woke Bertie, who had fallen asleep beneath the piano. He opened his eyes and stared at the scene of utter mayhem – the smashed bust, the ripped curtain, the broken tripod and three security guards chasing Clive, Camilla and Tiger round the hall.

Bertie turned to Douglas. 'Is it time to go?' he asked with a yawn.

Douglas nodded and the two of them headed for the door, where they were joined by Clive, Camilla and Tiger. The five cats scurried outside and ran for home.

'Do you think we made an impression?' asked Tiger.

The others laughed.

4

I'M a Star!

The following evening the five cats gathered in Bertie's front garden. They sat on the wall waiting for the paper boy to deliver news of the photo shoot.

'I hope I'm the one that's chosen,' said Tiger. 'When I've been on TV, people will recognize me everywhere I go. They'll want to stroke me and give me presents.'

'I won't let them touch me,' said Camilla, shuddering at the thought. 'When I'm famous, I'll be carried everywhere in a luxurious basket. People can look, but they can't touch.'

Clive jumped down from the wall and wandered up the path. He dipped a paw in a puddle of water and then made a damp pawprint on the ground.

'When I'm famous, I shall be happy to give everybody my paw-tograph,' he said.

'Don't build your hopes up,' said Bertie. 'There were hundreds of cats at the town hall. Any one of them could be chosen.'

'Bertie's right,' said Douglas. 'And even if one of us is lucky enough to be selected, it will hardly be a great way to become famous.'

'What do you mean?' asked Tiger.

'We'd simply be filmed eating, sleeping and

sitting around the house. Do you really want to be famous just for that?'

'I don't care what I'm famous for,' said Clive. 'I just want to be a celebrity.'

'Me too,' said Camilla.

'And me,' said Tiger.

'How sad,' mumbled Bertie.

'I once met a cat who had saved his owner's life,' said Douglas. 'He'd woken her when the house was on fire. That cat was in the newspapers and on the television. He became famous because he'd done something worthwhile.'

'Bully for him,' said Camilla. 'I just want to be famous, and when I am you'll all be really jealous.'

'I don't think any of us would be jealous,' said Douglas. 'We'd be really pleased for you.' He looked at the others. 'Wouldn't we?'

Nobody answered.

'I don't think we should be jealous,' insisted Douglas. 'Let's agree that if one of us is chosen we'll all remain friends. Friends for ever.'

Still the others were silent.

'We wouldn't let a silly TV programme come between us, would we?' asked Douglas. 'Whatever happens, surely we'll all stay friends.'

'Friends for ever!' shouted Tiger. He turned to Camilla. 'Friends for ever, Camilla?'

Camilla nodded. 'Friends for ever.'

'Clive?'

'Friends for ever.'

'Bertie?'

'Most certainly. Friends for ever.'

'Here comes the paper boy!' shouted Camilla.

The five cats watched as the boy worked his way up the road towards them. When he opened Bertie's front gate they rushed to him and swarmed around his feet. He'd never known such a welcome. The boy stopped for a moment to stroke each of them in turn and then walked up the path and shoved a newspaper through the letterbox.

The cats rushed to the back of the house, piled through the cat flap and charged up the hall.

Clive and Camilla pounced on the newspaper which was lying on the floor behind the front door. They frantically flicked through the

pages, glancing quickly at the words and
pictures. They stopped sharply on page eleven.
Clive read out the headline.

'Do you own this cat?'

Beneath it was a picture of Bertie, fast asleep.

Camilla read the article as quickly as she
could. 'Television producers are urgently seeking
the owner of this cat after it was chosen from

hundreds of hopefuls to feature in a new television programme. "We are desperate to find this cat," said TV producer Julian Jones. "He is everything we're looking for. An ordinary cat with star potential!"'

The cats looked at each other in amazement.

'I'm going to be a star,' said Bertie quietly. Then he shouted at the top of his voice, 'I'm going to be a star!'

'Congratulations,' said Douglas.

'Well done,' said Tiger.

Clive and Camilla weren't so generous. They leaped on the newspaper and ripped it to shreds.

5

Lights! Cameras! Action!

Mr and Mrs Spriggs contacted the TV company as soon as a neighbour showed them Bertie's photograph in the newspaper. Mrs Spriggs was delighted at the thought of her darling pet becoming a star. Mr Spriggs was equally delighted at the thought of being paid for it. He never normally bothered with Bertie – the first time he'd spoken to him that week was when he'd given him a kick up the backside after finding the ripped newspaper.

'Bloomin' fat cat!'

As soon as Mr Spriggs realized Bertie was about to appear on TV, he suddenly became very fond of him. He even went so far as to give him a cuddle.

'Going to make us rich, you are!'

Bertie stayed indoors for the next two days. During that time Clive, Camilla, Douglas and Tiger hung around in his front garden waiting for Mr and Mrs Spriggs to leave the house. When they eventually did go out, the four cats let themselves into Bertie's kitchen through the cat flap.

Tiger was full of questions. 'When do you start filming, Bertie?'

'Later this morning.'

'When will you be on TV?'

'The programme will be on in a few weeks.'

'Do they want any other cats to be in the programme?'

'No. There won't be any other cats starring alongside me. So, if that's why you're all here, I'm sorry to disappoint you.'

'We came to see how you are,' said Douglas. 'We haven't seen you for a while.'

'My owners don't want me to go out of the house in case I get dirty or come to any harm. Wouldn't that be terrible?'

'Terrible,' said Clive quietly. 'Terribly funny.'

Camilla sniggered.

'They'll be back soon,' said Bertie. 'They've gone to buy me a new collar. I think they're treating themselves to some new clothes as well.'

'Why?' asked Tiger.

'They want to look their best if they're caught on camera. I think they've started spending their fee before they've got it. And why not? It's going to change their lives as well as mine.'

'Can we stay and watch the filming?' asked Tiger.

'No, no, no,' said Bertie. 'In fact, you'd better go now. I want to have a little snooze before I start work.'

Clive, Camilla, Douglas and Tiger filed out through the cat flap.

'Good luck,' shouted Douglas.

The four cats wandered to the front of the house and sat on the garden wall. After about half an hour, Mr and Mrs Spriggs returned loaded up with bags and parcels. A short while later, a big green van pulled up. A young man jumped out and rushed to Bertie's front door.

It was opened by Mr and Mrs Spriggs, who were wearing their new outfits. They shook hands with the young man as he introduced himself.

'Julian Jones, director and producer of *Paws for Thought.*'

Mr and Mrs Spriggs showed him inside.

The four cats ran across the front garden, jumped onto the window sill and peered through the window. They could hardly believe their eyes. Bertie was parading around the lounge wearing a magnificent jewelled collar.

Julian swept Bertie off his feet and kissed him

on the nose.

'The star of the show!' he said. 'As soon as I saw you, I knew you were the one. All the others were desperate for attention, but you were a real cool cat.' Julian turned to Mr and Mrs Spriggs. 'It was as if it was too much trouble for him to open his eyes to have his photo taken!'

By now, two ladies and a man had unloaded the van. The four cats watched as reel after reel of fat cable was taken into the house together with various lamps, a camera, a small TV screen, some headphones and a huge microphone on the end of a pole.

Julian introduced his crew to Mr and Mrs Spriggs.

'This is Jeff, my sound operator. I call him Big Ears. My camera operator is Stephanie and this is my darling assistant, Patsy. Together we're known as the Fantastic Four. What we lack in numbers, we make up for with talent!'

Julian clicked his fingers and the four television makers swung into action. Stephanie and Big Ears began to set up their equipment while Julian paced around the lounge, deep in thought. Patsy turned her attention to Bertie.

Outside the four cats watched open-mouthed as Bertie was given a makeover.

'She's brushing his teeth!' shrieked Camilla.

The others shook their heads in disbelief.

'And now she's giving him a manicure!'

'A what?' said Tiger.

'She's trimming and polishing his claws!'

'I thought they were supposed to be filming the life of an ordinary cat,' said Douglas.

'She's grooming him now!' yelled Camilla. 'Look! Fluffing up his fur as if he's a show cat!'

Bertie was enjoying all the fuss. When he spotted the others watching, he turned his back on them.

Clive was furious. 'Who does he think he is?'

Julian clapped his hands. 'I think we'll start by having Bertie catch a mouse,' he said.

'We don't have mice!' said Mrs Spriggs.

Patsy held up a little cage. 'You do now!'

Patsy opened the cage and took out a tiny white mouse. Julian lifted Bertie into his basket and placed it by the fireplace.

'When I shout "action" I want the mouse to

be released,' he said. 'It will run across the floor and we'll observe Bertie's transformation from dopey pet to wild animal. He'll pounce like a ferocious, untamed creature!'

The four cats were watching carefully. 'This should be a laugh,' said Clive.

Camilla nodded. 'Bertie's never caught a

mouse in his life. He's too slow to catch a cold.'

'Let's make some television!' shouted Julian. Big Ears, Stephanie and Patsy took up their positions. 'Quiet everybody. Thank you. And… action!'

The little mouse scurried across the carpet. Julian stroked his chin in eager anticipation of the drama that was about to unfold. The mouse was now next to Bertie's basket. Everybody held their breath waiting for Bertie to make his move, but Bertie didn't move at all – he was fast asleep.

Stephanie glanced at Julian, who signalled she should continue to film. The mouse sniffed around the basket and then climbed inside and snuggled up to Bertie.

Outside the other cats were laughing their heads off.

'Cut!' shouted Julian.

Bertie woke with a start.

'Now he's for it,' whispered Camilla.

Clive was happy to agree. 'They'll realize he's useless and give him the sack.'

Julian grabbed Bertie, picked him up and gave him a big kiss.

'Brilliant! Better than I could have dreamed!

I knew this cat was something special!'

Everybody nodded and agreed.

Clive jumped down from the window sill. 'I can't stand any more of this,' he said.

'Neither can I,' said Camilla.

She leaped to the ground and followed Clive round the side of the house.

Inside, everybody had crowded around Bertie. He'd never been stroked by so many people at once.

6

Bust Up

Douglas and Tiger continued to watch the programme makers in action. Julian had set up a scene in which Bertie was supposed to chase after a small ball.

'Let's observe the cat at play,' he said. 'We can learn about his sense of fun.'

On Julian's cue, Patsy rolled the ball across the lounge. Bertie ambled over to it and sat on it. When anybody tried to retrieve the ball, Bertie let out a loud hiss and refused to budge.

'I love it!' shouted Julian. 'This cat is simply full of surprises!'

Once again, Bertie was mobbed by his adoring fans.

Outside, Tiger continued to dream of a chance of stardom.

'If we hang about we might get noticed,' he said. 'We might be – '

'Listen!' said Douglas.

Tiger stopped talking and pricked up his ears. A high pitched yowl echoed around the neighbourhood.

'It's the emergency signal!' said Tiger. 'It must be Clive or Camilla.'

'Something terrible must have happened,' said Douglas.

The two cats dropped to the ground in an instant. They ran along the side of the house and into the back garden. Clive and Camilla were sitting beneath the apple tree. Douglas and Tiger sprinted towards them.

'Are you all right?' asked Douglas urgently. 'What's happened?'

'I'll tell you as soon as we're all here,' said Clive. 'We must wait for Bertie.'

'Bertie won't be able to come,' said Tiger. 'He's filming.'

'He'll be here,' said Clive. 'When any of us hears the emergency signal, we must stop whatever we're doing and meet immediately.

That's the rule.'

Clive sounded the alarm once again. Tiger looked anxiously towards the house, but there was no sign of Bertie.

'If he doesn't come he'll be thrown out of the Courageous Cats' Club,' said Camilla.

'That seems a bit harsh,' said Douglas.

Tiger agreed. 'He can't come if he's working.'

'Sadly, his work appears to be more important than his friends,' said Clive. 'He's ignored the emergency call and broken the rule. It is with deep regret I must announce that Bertie is – '

'Bertie is what?' said Bertie.

'Hurray!' shouted Tiger. 'You made it!'

'Well done,' said Douglas. 'Did you stop filming so you could come to the meeting?'

'We've finished for today,' said Bertie.

'Finished?' snapped Camilla. 'You've only just started!'

'It's exhausting work being a TV star.'

Douglas turned to Clive. 'So what's the emergency? Why did you sound the alarm?'

'Erm...' For a moment Clive was stuck for words. 'Erm... Because... Because I was testing it. Yes, that's right. I was testing it!'

'Why?' asked Tiger.

'To check everybody could hear it. And the test seems to have been very successful.'

'Are you sure it was the alarm you were testing?' said Bertie. 'And not me?'

'What do you mean?' asked Tiger.

'I think Clive sounded the alarm because he thought I wouldn't be able to come to the meeting.'

'Why would he want to do that?' asked Tiger, confused.

'So he could throw me out of the club.'

'Why would he want to do that?' asked Tiger again.

'Because he's jealous! Jealous that I'm the one who is going to be on TV. Jealous that I'm going to be famous!'

Clive laughed. 'The only thing you'll be famous for is being fat!'

'I might be fat,' said Bertie. 'But at least I've got a tail!'

Clive got to his feet and walked slowly towards Bertie. 'What did you say?'

Douglas stepped between them. He was worried there was going to be a fight.

'Calm down. Friends for ever, remember?'

Bertie turned his back on Clive. 'I don't know if I want to be friends with somebody who could play a rotten trick like that.'

'I don't want to be friends with *you*!' shouted Clive.

'See if I care. I'll have lots of *new* friends soon. My owners said they're going to take me to the Kitty Salon every week.'

'You'll need some new friends,' said Clive. 'Because I'm kicking you out of the Courageous

Cats' Club!'

'I don't want to be in it any more, anyway.'

Bertie headed back towards the house.

'Good riddance to fat rubbish!' shouted Clive.

The four cats watched as Bertie squeezed through his cat flap.

'You can't throw him out of the club,' said Tiger quietly. 'He hasn't done anything wrong.'

'I can do what I like,' said Clive.

'If anybody should be thrown out, it's you,' said Tiger. 'You sounded the alarm when there wasn't an emergency. You broke a rule.'

'Fine!' shouted Clive. 'I've had enough of the stupid club, anyway.'

'Me too,' said Camilla. 'Come on Clive, let's go and start a new club of our own.'

Clive and Camilla crawled under the hedge and disappeared.

'Wait!' shouted Tiger. 'I didn't mean it. You've not really been thrown out of the club!'

'There is no club!' yelled Clive. 'It's finished! For ever!'

7

Clive Gets a Shock

The TV crew arrived early the following
morning and began to set up their equipment
in Bertie's kitchen. Tiger and Douglas positioned
themselves on the window sill at the back of the
house so as not to miss anything. A few minutes
later, Clive and Camilla appeared.

'Hi Clive,' said Douglas. 'Hi Camilla.'

They ignored him.

'Do you want to come and sit with us?' asked
Tiger. 'They'll be filming another scene soon.'

'Not if I've got anything to do with it,' said
Clive quietly.

Camilla sniggered.

In the house, Julian was very excited. 'I've
had an idea,' he said. 'It's rather a good one,
even if I say so myself. I'm going to test the cat's

intelligence!'

'I'm afraid Bertie's not very clever,' said Mrs Spriggs.

'He's an idiot,' said Mr Spriggs.

Julian showed Big Ears where to position himself with the microphone and then instructed Stephanie to set up a big lamp on a stand outside the house so as to throw some extra light into the kitchen. Patsy meanwhile was preparing Bertie for another session in front of the camera.

'Attention, everybody,' said Julian. 'As you can see, I've placed three saucers on the floor. In a moment, I shall put a piece of cat meat on saucer number two.'

Bertie licked his lips.

'Saucers number one and three will remain empty,' said Julian. 'I will then cover each saucer with a cloth so the food is hidden from view. Bertie will be taken into the hall. On my shout of "action", Patsy will allow him into the room and we'll see how long it takes him to find the meat.'

'He'll be able to smell it,' said Mrs Spriggs.

'I thought of that,' said Julian. 'Each cloth has

been scented with fish to confuse him.'

Patsy picked up Bertie and took him out of the room. Bertie was looking forward to the test, but he didn't know what it would prove – he knew where the meat would be, because Julian had just announced it.

'Let's make some television!' shouted Julian. Big Ears and Stephanie took up their positions. 'Quiet, everybody. Thank you. And... action!'

Patsy opened the door and Bertie wandered in. He headed straight for saucer number two, tugged the piece of cloth to one side and ate the food.

Everybody gasped.

The experiment was repeated. Once again, Bertie immediately went to the correct saucer and helped himself to the food.

'Incredible!' cried Julian. 'This cat is truly incredible!'

Bertie was baffled by all the excitement he was causing, but happy to continue with the test all day if required.

'Let's try saucer number two again,' said Julian.

Patsy picked up Bertie and took him into the hall.

Clive had been watching all of this from the back doorstep. The door was slightly ajar to allow a cable to run from a socket inside the house to the huge lamp which had been placed outside the window. The big bright bulb was shining into the kitchen, illuminating Bertie's performance. Clive flicked the cable with a paw.

'What are you doing?' asked Tiger.

'I'm about to put an end to Bertie's TV career,' said Clive.

He took a closer look at the cable.

'Leave that alone,' warned Douglas.

'Don't tell me what to do,' said Clive.

In the kitchen, everybody was applauding –
Bertie had picked the correct saucer once again.

'When people see this, they'll be amazed!'
shrieked Julian. 'The cat's a genius!'

Clive grabbed the cable in his mouth.

'It's dangerous to touch anything electrical,'
said Douglas.

Clive ignored him and bit into the cable. There
was a spark, a fizzle and then a very loud bang.
Clive shot into the air, his fur standing on end. A
moment later, he hit the ground with a thud.

'Clive, are you all right?' asked Camilla
urgently.

Clive opened his mouth to say something, but
nothing came out.

Douglas and Tiger jumped down from the
window sill.

'Are you hurt?' asked Douglas.

Clive didn't answer. Instead, he carefully got
to his feet, walked slowly down the garden and
staggered into the bushes. The other cats
followed.

Inside the house, there was great confusion.

'What happened to the lamp, Stephanie?'

asked Julian.

'I'm not sure. I think we've blown a fuse somewhere.'

Outside, there was great concern.

'Clive, are you all right?' asked Tiger.

Clive shook his head slowly. 'I don't… I don't feel very well.'

Then he collapsed.

8

⠿

Tiger in the Spotlight

Clive lay on the ground, shaking.

'We need to get some help,' said Douglas urgently. 'I'll go back to the house. I'll attract somebody's attention. When they see Clive's hurt, they'll call the vet.'

'Thanks, Douglas,' said Clive feebly. 'But I'm afraid… I'm afraid it's too late for that.'

'What do you mean?' said Camilla.

'I don't know if I can hang on much longer,' gasped Clive. 'I think I've used up the last of my nine lives.'

'No!' said Tiger.

'Goodbye. And thanks for being such good friends.'

Tiger, Douglas and Camilla didn't know what to say.

'I just wish… I just wish I could say goodbye to Bertie,' said Clive sadly.

'Let's use the emergency signal!' said Tiger. 'I'm sure he'll come.'

'I doubt it,' said Douglas. 'He'll think it's another trick.'

Clive nodded slowly. 'You're right.'

'It's all Bertie's fault,' said Camilla. 'If he

hadn't got the job on TV, this wouldn't have happened.'

'It's my fault,' said Clive. 'And I can't bear to think my last words to him were filled with such hatred. I'm determined to apologize.'

He struggled to his feet, and took a few unsteady steps before collapsing again.

'It's no use. I'll never make it.'

'I'll go and fetch Bertie,' said Tiger. 'I'll tell him what's happened.'

'Would you do that?' asked Clive.

'Of course.'

Tiger dashed up the garden. He didn't slow down as he approached the house. He took a huge leap and dived head first through Bertie's cat flap. He skidded across the tiled floor and looked anxiously around the kitchen. It was empty. The door which led to the rest of the house was closed. Tiger ran to it, stood on his hind legs and leaned against it with his front paws. He let out the loudest miaow he could manage. It did the trick. The door opened and in came Julian and Patsy. Tiger tried to squeeze past them, but Julian bent down and picked him up.

'Hello. Where did you come from?'

'He's been hanging around the house for ages,' said Patsy. 'Shall I put him outside?'

Julian shook his head. 'No. He's given me an idea. We'll have a scene with two cats. We'll let them play together and observe how Bertie gets on with this little fellow.'

The thought of being on TV was enough to make Tiger's right ear begin to twitch. But then he remembered Clive and knew he must put his friend before any thoughts of stardom.

Julian handed Tiger to Patsy before rushing to tell the others about his latest idea.

Patsy gave Tiger a cuddle. 'You don't need much beauty treatment, do you? You're gorgeous already.'

She placed Tiger on the kitchen table and began to give him a makeover. At first Tiger wouldn't stand still. He was eager to find Bertie and tell him what had happened, but, as Patsy began to brush his fur, Tiger gave up the struggle and decided to wait until Bertie came into the room.

The hairbrush tickled and Tiger started to

purr. He lay down and rolled onto his back. The grooming seemed to go on for ever and Tiger loved every minute of it.

'The viewers will love you,' said Patsy.

Tiger closed his eyes and imagined a crowd of adoring fans calling his name, taking his photograph and trying to get near enough to stroke him.

'Shall I polish your claws?' asked Patsy. 'Then you'll look *really* glamorous.'

Tiger jumped to his feet and allowed the pampering to continue.

It will only take a few minutes to film the scene, he thought. *And as soon it's finished, I'll tell Bertie about Clive's accident.*

At that moment, Julian returned with Bertie in his arms. Bertie was shocked to see Tiger having a manicure.

'Could you come through to the dining room, Patsy?' said Julian. 'I'm going to shoot the next scene in there. Leave the cats in here to get to know each other.'

Bertie waited for Julian and Patsy to leave and then spoke quietly.

'What are you doing here?'

'They want me to be in the next scene with you,' said Tiger excitedly.

'I might not want you to be in it,' said Bertie. 'I'm the star of the show.'

'Please, Bertie. It's my chance to become famous. We could play a game. What about hide-and-seek? I'll tell you where I'm going to hide and when you find me, you'll look really clever.'

Bertie thought about it.

'Or *you* can hide,' said Tiger. 'I'll pretend I can't find you. What do you think?'

'You can hide,' said Bertie. 'That way the camera will be looking at me most of the time.'

'Whatever you say.' Tiger climbed into the vegetable rack. 'Shall I hide in here?'

Suddenly, Douglas crashed through the cat flap.

'Bertie, have you seen Tiger?'

'He's hiding behind that cauliflower.'

'What?' Douglas spotted Tiger peering out from the vegetable rack. 'What are you doing? Have you told Bertie what happened?'

Tiger suddenly felt thoroughly embarrassed.

'Clive's had an accident,' said Douglas. 'He's hurt himself badly.'

'What's that got to do with me?' said Bertie.

'He wants to apologize to you and say goodbye.'

'Say goodbye?'

'The accident was very nasty. He's certain he won't recover.'

'I'm sorry to hear that,' said Bertie.

'He thought you might come and see him.'

'After the rotten trick he played yesterday? No chance.'

'So you won't come?' asked Douglas.

'No, I won't.'

'Shall I give him a message?'

'No.'

'You don't have a message for a dying friend?'

'He's not my friend any more. Now, if you'll excuse me, I have to rehearse with Tiger.'

Tiger scrambled out of the vegetable rack. 'What am I doing?' he said. 'Rehearsing for a TV programme when I should be with Clive. He's been my friend since the day I was born. He was the first friend I ever had.' Tiger stood by Douglas's side. 'I'm coming with you, Douglas. Are you sure you won't come, Bertie? Clive's been a good friend to you too, hasn't he?'

'In the past he has, yes.'

'Good friends are very hard to find,' said Douglas. 'If you're lucky enough to have some, you should do everything you can to keep them.'

'What if we never saw him again?' said Tiger. 'Imagine if we stayed here to do the TV programme and then found out that...' Tiger's words trailed away to nothing.

'Is your fame more important than a dying friend?' asked Douglas.

Bertie thought for a moment. Then he shook his head. 'No,' he said quietly.

'So you'll come and see him?'

Bertie nodded.

Tiger dived through the cat flap. Bertie climbed through after him. It was a tight squeeze and Douglas had to give him a shove from behind. Bertie popped out the other side. Douglas followed.

'I just hope we're not too late,' he said.

The three cats ran down the garden.

9

Friends or Fame?

As Bertie, Tiger and Douglas approached the bushes they could hear Clive and Camilla chatting.

'You were brilliant, Clive,' said Camilla. 'You even had *me* fooled for a moment. Are you sure you're not hurt?'

'Not at all,' replied Clive. 'I told you I should have been on TV. You'll never see better acting than that.'

'It certainly looked dramatic!'

'Did you see Douglas's face?' asked Clive. 'He was more shocked than me!'

They both laughed.

'And what about Tiger?' said Camilla. 'I thought he was going to burst into tears!'

'I was sure he'd go for Bertie,' said Clive.

'I knew if I could convince him I was about to die, he'd go and fetch fatso.'

'But will he come?'

'I hope so. I'm running out of ideas to ruin his television pro – '

Clive nearly choked on his words. Bertie, Tiger and Douglas were standing a few feet away. They'd heard everything.

Douglas was furious. 'You should be ashamed of yourself!'

Tiger couldn't believe it. 'You mean... You mean it was another trick? There was nothing wrong with you, Clive?'

Clive didn't answer.

'It was another attempt to ruin things for Bertie,' said Douglas. 'All Clive wants to do is stop Bertie from appearing on TV.'

'And he's succeeded,' said Bertie.

'What are you talking about?' asked Tiger. 'You're going to go back and carry on filming, aren't you?'

'No.'

'Why not?'

'Douglas has reminded me how important my friends are. They're much more important than being famous.' Bertie sat down. 'As soon as I got the job on TV I didn't care about any of you. I was interested only in myself. I'm sorry.'

'It's me that should be sorry,' said Clive quietly. 'I've behaved so badly. I was jealous of you. We all agreed we wouldn't let that happen, but it did.'

'Jealousy is a horrible thing,' said Douglas.

Clive nodded slowly. 'I can't believe how much I've changed in the space of a few days.'

'I've changed too,' said Bertie. 'Not only my behaviour, but my appearance as well!' He laughed. 'Look at me! A fancy collar and a hairdo to match.'

Clive, Camilla and Douglas smiled, but Tiger couldn't bring himself to do the same. He knew that he too had come very close to choosing fame above a friend.

'I think you should go back to your filming, Bertie,' said Clive. 'Enjoy it, and I hope you're successful.'

'That TV programme nearly split up the Courageous Cats' Club,' said Bertie. 'I don't want anything more to do with it.'

By now, Bertie's owners were out in the garden. They were becoming concerned about his absence.

'Bertie, darling!' shouted Mrs Spriggs. 'Where are you?'

Mr Spriggs shouted even louder. 'Come here, fatso!'

Clive stared at the ground. He couldn't bear to look Bertie in the face. 'I called you names,' he said. 'I'm sorry.'

'We both said things we're sorry about,' said Bertie. 'But we can put it all behind us if we want to.'

'Friends for ever?' asked Douglas.

'Friends for ever,' said Bertie.

'Friends for ever,' said Clive.

'Come on, Bertie!' shouted Mrs Spriggs. 'We can't film without you!'

'Come in, you daft cat!' shouted Mr Spriggs. 'If we can't film, we won't get our money!'

'What are you going to do, Bertie?' asked Douglas. 'They'll find you if you stay here.'

'I'll have to lie low for a while. Do you think I could hide in your shed?'

'Of course,' said Douglas. 'If you're sure that's what you want.'

'What I want is to get things back to how they were before.'

'That's what I want too,' said Clive.

10

∴

Welcome Home

The cats ran through the undergrowth to Douglas's garden. There, they climbed into the shed through a broken window and stayed out of sight.

Bertie's owners were still pleading for him to return.

'Come on, Bertie!' shouted Mrs Spriggs. 'I've got a big bowl of fish for you!'

'Come on, Bertie!' shouted Mr Spriggs. 'I've got a big boot for your backside!'

Their calls continued for the rest of the morning. At lunchtime they stopped and the neighbourhood was quiet.

Clive left the shed and went to see what was going on. A few minutes later he was back.

'The TV crew has packed up and gone home.'

'Good,' said Tiger. 'That means Bertie can go home too.'

'No,' said Bertie. 'I'm going to stay here. They may come back tomorrow and the whole thing will start again.'

'Are you going to spend the night here?' asked Camilla.

'That's right.'

'It won't be very comfortable.'

'I don't care. I'm not going home until I'm certain the TV crew has gone for ever.'

Bertie was as good as his word. Two days and nights he stayed in the shed. The only food he had were the scraps that the others managed to take to him. The only times he ventured outside were under cover of darkness and even then, he didn't stray far from the shed.

Each day and night Mr and Mrs Spriggs continued to call for Bertie. Mrs Spriggs was growing more and more upset, and there were times when Bertie wanted to go to her. He was missing her so much. He was missing his nice comfortable basket too, not to mention three good meals a day with snacks in between.

On the third morning, Bertie was very nearly discovered. Douglas rushed to the shed and warned him that Mr and Mrs Spriggs were looking in everybody's shed and garage in case Bertie had become trapped.

Within minutes they could hear voices. Bertie and Douglas crawled under a plastic sheet and held their breath. The shed door opened.

'I hope we find him today,' said Mrs Spriggs.

'So do I,' said her husband. 'You heard what Julian said, if he doesn't show up today, that's it. The filming is cancelled and so is our fee!'

'I'm not bothered about the filming or the fee,' replied Mrs Spriggs. 'I just want my baby back.'

Mr Spriggs rummaged among the garden tools and had a look inside an old cupboard.

'He's not here. Come on, let's try next door.'

After a few minutes, the two cats crawled out from their hiding place.

'That was a close call,' said Douglas.

'Yes, but I'm safe now,' said Bertie. 'All being well, I'll be able to go home tomorrow.'

The following morning, Douglas, Clive, Camilla and Tiger escorted Bertie through the neighbouring gardens back to his house.

'I'm going to spend all day in bed,' said Bertie. 'The only time I'll get out of my basket is to have something to eat.'

'Things really will be back to normal,' said Tiger.

The others laughed.

The five cats crawled under the garden fence, trotted past the apple tree and headed for the back door. Mrs Spriggs was staring out of the kitchen window. When she saw Bertie, her face filled with joy.

'My baby! He's come home!'

She ran to the door and flung it open. In no time at all Mr Spriggs was there too.

'My precious has come back!' he said.

He ran down the garden, with his arms open wide. He grabbed Bertie and swept him off his feet.

'My little treasure!'

Mr Spriggs tugged at Bertie's collar and ripped it off. He kissed each of the jewels one by one.

'It's so good to have you back, my precious!'

He dropped Bertie on the ground.

'What are you doing?' shouted Mrs Spriggs.

'At least I'll be able to get my money back on this collar!' snarled Mr Spriggs.

'But what about Bertie?'

'That cat is not putting one paw inside our house ever again!'

Mr Spriggs bundled Mrs Spriggs inside and slammed the door. He opened a window and

yelled at the top of his voice.

'Clear off, you useless moggy! I could have been rich but for you!'

'Please let him in,' pleaded Mrs Spriggs.

Mr Spriggs slammed the window so hard that the glass nearly shattered.

Douglas, Clive, Camilla and Tiger ran to Bertie.

'Are you all right?' asked Tiger.

'They don't want me any more,' said Bertie quietly.

'I'm sure you'll be allowed back in the house in a couple of days or so,' said Clive.

'Yes,' said Camilla. 'You just need to give it a bit more time.'

'Look!' shouted Tiger.

Mr Spriggs had reappeared in the kitchen with his toolbox and a piece of hardboard. A few seconds later, there was a loud hammering sound. Mr Spriggs was boarding up the cat flap.

'I'm homeless,' said Bertie, with tears in his eyes. 'I'm an abandoned cat.'

The others sat down next to their friend.

'You can come and live at my house,' said Douglas. 'I'm sure you'll be made very welcome.'

'We'll all come and visit you,' said Tiger.

'I want to live in my own house,' said Bertie sadly. 'I want things to be just how they were.'

'And so they shall,' said Clive.

'How?' asked Camilla.

'I have a plan. All Courageous Cats to meet at midnight.'

11

Midnight Mission

As the town hall clock struck twelve, five cats scurried through the darkness and gathered beneath the apple tree in Bertie's garden.

'What's the plan, Clive?' said Douglas.

'We're going to give Mr Spriggs a night he'll never forget.'

'What do you mean?' asked Tiger.

'He always leaves the house very early in the morning to go to work,' said Clive. 'The one thing he'll want is a good night's sleep and that's the one thing he's not going to get.'

'What are we going to do?' asked Camilla.

'Firstly, we're going to take up our positions.'

Clive led the way to the back of the house and the five cats sat on the patio beneath the bedroom window. 'On the count of three, we'll

have a quick chorus from the Courageous Cats'
Club Choir,' said Clive. 'One… two… three…'

The cats began to wail and whine and to yelp
and yowl, their shrill shrieks filling the night air.
It wasn't long before the bedroom light went on.
A moment later, the bedroom window opened
and Mr Spriggs leaned out.

'Shut up, you moaning moggies!'

Clive raised a paw and the choir was silent.

The window closed and the light went off.

'We'll give him a few minutes to nod off again,' said Clive. 'Then we'll have an encore.'

And that's exactly what they did. Again the bedroom light went on. Again the window opened and again Mr Spriggs shouted at the cats. They were silent until they were satisfied he'd gone back to bed, and then they started singing again.

Once more the bedroom light went on, but this time it was followed by the bathroom light.

'Take cover, everybody,' said Clive. 'He's going for the old water trick.'

The cats hid in the bushes. The bathroom window opened and Mr Spriggs leaned out and threw the contents of a jug of water into the garden.

'Take that!' he yelled.

A few minutes later, the house was in darkness again, which was the cue for the cats to have another sing-song.

By now, Mr Spriggs was at the end of his tether. Wearing only his pyjamas, he raced downstairs and out of the kitchen door. He spotted five pairs of cat's eyes staring out from the blackness. Mr Spriggs charged down the garden. He didn't see the wheelbarrow in the dark. He tripped over it and landed head first in the compost heap.

Mrs Spriggs came running out of the house in her nightie.

'Cyril, are you all right?'

'No, I'm not all right!'

Mr Spriggs struggled to his feet, brushing grass cuttings from his hair.

'I've hardly had a wink of sleep and I've got to be up soon! If I catch those cats, I'll throttle them!'

'Perhaps it's Bertie,' said Mrs Spriggs. 'Perhaps it's his way of asking to be allowed in.'

'Well, it won't work!'

Mr and Mrs Spriggs went back inside the house.

'That's it for tonight,' said Clive. 'I reckon we'll have you back in your home by the end of the week, Bertie.'

The cats continued to meet at midnight every

night and proceeded to make Mr Spriggs's life an absolute misery.

They took it in turns to leap into the air and flick the front door knocker with a paw. Then they hid and watched as Mr Spriggs repeatedly came downstairs to see who was there.

The following night, the cats managed to get into the greenhouse. Clive climbed onto a shelf and pushed off a plant pot. It shattered on the ground. Mr Spriggs was out of the house in an instant, looking for an intruder. He didn't find one, of course. By the time Mr Spriggs was back in bed, the cats were back in the greenhouse, ready to repeat the exercise.

After a week of torment, Mr Spriggs was a physical wreck. The final straw came when the cats spent most of the night scratching the kitchen door. Mr Spriggs went downstairs five times to chase them away. On the sixth time he opened the door and stared into the garden. The cats stared back.

'You win,' he said wearily.

Mrs Spriggs appeared at her husband's side.

'Why don't we let Bertie back in the house?' she said. 'See if it puts a stop to the disturbances.'

'All right,' said Mr Spriggs with a yawn. 'Anything to get some sleep. If this carries on, I'm going to lose my job. The boss said if I nod off at work one more time, he'll give me the sack.'

Mr Spriggs shuffled into the house. He was

practically sleepwalking.

'Bertie!' shouted Mrs Spriggs. 'Come here, my darling!'

'We've done it,' whispered Clive. 'Well done, team.'

The cats congratulated each other on a successful mission.

'Good night, everybody,' said Bertie. 'And thanks for helping.'

'That's what friends are for,' said Clive.

Bertie scampered towards the house. Mrs Spriggs picked him up and gave him a big hug.

'Welcome home,' she said.

12

Friends for Ever

Tiger sat beneath the apple tree in Bertie's garden and let out a high-pitched yowl. In a matter of minutes, Clive, Camilla and Douglas were racing towards him.

'What's happened?' asked Clive

'What's the emergency?' asked Camilla.

'Where's Bertie?' asked Douglas. 'Is he all right?'

'Bertie's not coming,' said Tiger.

'Why? What's happened to him?'

'He's on the television right now!'

Clive, Camilla and Douglas could hardly believe it.

'He really did make it onto the TV?' asked Camilla.

'Yes,' said Tiger.

'Good for him,' said Clive.

'I know it's not really an emergency, but I thought you'd all want to see him.'

'Of course we do.'

Tiger led the way towards Bertie's house. 'Mr and Mrs Spriggs have gone out,' he explained. 'And the cat flap is open again.'

The four cats jumped through it. They ran through the kitchen into the lounge. The television was in the corner of the room. Sitting on top of it was Bertie.

'I'm on the television!' he shouted. 'Would anybody like my paw-tograph?'

Clive, Camilla and Douglas laughed.

'I'm going to be on the television too,' said Tiger.

He climbed onto a chair and leaped onto the TV set.

'Me too,' said Camilla.

'And me,' said Clive.

Douglas wasn't going to be the only one to miss out. 'Is there room for another one?'

The five cats squeezed onto the top of the TV.

'We did it!' said Bertie. 'We managed to get

onto the television and remain friends.'

'Friends for ever?' asked Douglas.

'Friends for ever!' they shouted.

Also available from Lion Children's Books

The Courageous Cats' Club
Steve Wood

Two fun-filled animal stories about friendship, bravery and much more.

Sticks and Stones

Douglas is lonely and missing his old home. Then he hears about the Courageous Cats' Club. Douglas is shy but he thinks he might be brave enough to join them and make some new friends. But things don't turn out quite as he had hoped.

The Beast of the Night

Something strange is terrorizing the neighbourhood. It's noisy and hungry and messy, and the cats are fed up with getting the blame for everything it does. At last they pluck up courage to face the beast and set a trap – with surprising results.

ISBN-13: 978 0 7459 4832 4
ISBN-10: 0 7459 4832 4

All Lion books are available from your local bookshop, or can be ordered via our website or from Marston Book Services. For a free catalogue, showing the complete list of titles available, please contact:

Customer Services
Marston Book Services
PO Box 269
Abingdon
Oxon
OX14 4YN

Tel: 01235 465500
Fax: 01235 465555

Our website can be found at:
www.lionhudson.com